CW00956893

THE LAST DAYS OF
BILLY PATCH

In their physical appearance the Branston brothers displayed an obvious family resemblance, but underneath the skin, they couldn't have been more different. Joe was a loser, a hobo on horseback, not above swamping saloons for cents as he bummed his way across the west.

Billy was a go-getter, making it with the girls; the young kid with the Midas touch, setting up his own ranch in Texas.

When Joe found he couldn't even earn a few pesos in Mexico, he decided to ride north and look up his kid brother. So, when he finally made it to Brightwater, he was full of expectations that his life was to take a turn. It changed direction all right, but not in the way he expected.

The Last Days of Billy Patch

B.J. HOLMES

A Black Horse Western

ROBERT HALE · LONDON

ISBN 0 7090 4808 4

Robert Hale Limited
Clerkenwell House
Clerkenwell Green
London EC1R 0HT

For Jean

Photoset in North Wales by
Derek Doyle & Associates, Mold, Clwyd.
Printed in Great Britain by
St Edmundsbury Press Ltd, Bury St Edmunds, Suffolk.
Bound by WBC Bookbinders Ltd, Bridgend, Glamorgan.

Prologue

'Hey, Janacek,' Sergeant Morley shouted. His eyes, set in the rough ugly face, had the gleam long familiar to his men. 'Know how many Polacks it takes to shoe a horse?'

The young Ranger of Polish origin had learned long since not to react to the sergeant's verbal spikes. 'No, Sarge,' Janacek called back, 'but I feel you're gonna tell me.'

'Five,' the sergeant went on, loud enough to be heard above the creak of saddle leather and the clop of hooves on sand. 'One to nail the shoe on the hoof and four to hold the hoss upside down!'

The riders around Private Janacek guffawed at their sergeant's punch line. Janacek smiled too, partly at the funny side and partly in good-humoured contempt. Contempt for the sergeant with a wooden block for a head yet the uninformed arrogance to assume that it was the Polish race that was without intelligence. But he took it without rancour because he knew the sarge didn't mean it personal. The non-com took a rise out of all his men on occasion. Even more, he wasn't above laughing at himself when he'd done something stupid. It was just his way. He found humour in anything.

Ahead, Lieutenant Sinclair glanced back. Six feet of relaxed sinewy muscle, he rode easy in the saddle. His non-com's clowning had been voiced loud enough to reach his ears. 'Sergeant,' he shouted. 'I just don't know how you can be so jocular at a time like this.' There was no reprimand in his voice. His sergeant's demeanour was an asset and he had the sense to know it: a rare balance of discipline and rough humanity that had the respect of his men. The ranks jumped when he told them to. On the other hand, he could raise genuine laughs among them with the natural flair to know the right time to do so, taking the edge off bad situations.

The non-com shrugged. 'You gotta keep in touch with the lighter side of life, sir. Otherwise you go nuts.'

There was truth in that. You needed some safety valve after what they'd seen over the last few days: burnt-out homes, ripped-up women, dead kids, unspeakable mutilations. The Comanche had been quiet for years. Then a bunch of renegades had cut loose from their reservation up in Indian Territory, raising Cain in southern Texas. As far as could be made out, there was no sign yet of a general uprising but the handful of mavericks, seemingly intent on nothing but mindless violence, had to be stopped. It was a stroke of luck that a detachment of D Company were in the territory. As soon as the news had come through, a unit of eighteen Rangers headed by Captain Fairfax had been sent south to restore the white man's version of order.

For a spell there was little sound other than the creak and jingle of harnesses. The terrain which the column of eighteen riders and half a dozen pack ponies traversed was bleak, merely broken here and there by twisted mesquite.

'Smoke,' Morley muttered suddenly. 'I can smell smoke. Just a hint, hanging on the air.'

The Rangers around him turned in their saddles, scanning all quarters. Nothing but gravel, brush and bunch grass. And no smoke.

'I'm gonna tell the lieutenant,' the sergeant said, spurring forward along the slowly moving column. He relayed his observation to the officer. Sinclair could see nothing suspicious nor detect smoke but he had faith in the non-com. Joel Sinclair and Bill Morley had been together a long time, having enlisted in the Rangers together at the end of the war. 'What breeze there is, is coming from the west,' he said, wheeling his horse to one side. The column continued on its way as he took out his binoculars and focused them on the western horizon. The land rose to a ridge but there was nothing untoward.

'It's there again,' Morley said, his head rising and his nostrils twitching. 'Smoke as sure as hell.'

'That's good enough for me,' Sinclair said after further contemplation. He returned the eyeglasses to their leather holder and nudged his horse forward. Ahead Captain Fairfax was raising his hand, signalling a halt as the unit scout was in view. By the time Sinclair made the head of the column the captain was in discussion with the scout.

The commanding officer was an old veteran

with grizzled beard and a no-nonsense look in his eye. 'The scout has cut sign to the north,' he said to his lieutenant as he reined in. 'Looks like the war party is swinging west.'

'I'm sure of it, sir,' Sinclair said. 'My sergeant's smelled smoke coming from the same direction. He's got a face like a bull mastiff and a sense of smell just as acute as the dog's.'

'That confirms it,' the captain said. He despatched the scout westward then swung his arm indicating the column to follow suit.

A mile further on they topped the ridge of the rising plain. Below they could see the scout investigating what remained of a small settlement of adobes. A wisp of smoke curled from the cavity of a mud jacal where a roof had been. The bloody carcasses of several cattle were scattered some distance off. Corral fences were broken and wagons upturned. Then, as the main contingent of Rangers worked their way down the grade, they could make out bodies.

'Jesus,' Sinclair breathed, making even ground and dismounting alongside the figure of an elderly man. He'd been gun-shot in the back of the head and then scalped. Sinclair couldn't help imagining the scenario. Some yards away was a crude hitchrail in the shade of a gnarled cottonwood. There would have been horses there, valuable prizes since taken by the Indians. Likely the old-timer had been trying to make it to a horse when they got him in the back of the head. Most of his clothing had been stripped and there were mutilations other than the scalping.

Sinclair was a brooding man. Like all the

Rangers in the unit he was becoming hardened to sights of mayhem such as lay before him but there came a time when enough was enough. He had a furlough coming up, postponed because of the current exercise. Hell, he needed the break. He needed to get back to his own wife and kids and remind himself there was an ordinary life out there, where ordinary things happened, like building swings for kids in the yard, playing cards with the guys in the saloon, talking about crops, horse racing at the annual fair; the luxury of a soft bed with his arms round his wife.

A voice snapped him out of it. 'Five dead.' It was the scout, first to the scene and reporting to the captain, himself now down from his horse and surveying the carnage. 'Three men, a woman and a child,' the scout went on. 'It's the work of Indians all right. You can tell by the way the victims were slaughtered.' The observation was unnecessary. 'Figure it's the same bunch of Comanches that we're after, sir.'

The captain handed his reins to his orderly and, along with his lieutenant, appraised the atrocities while the scout made a wide circle of the site. Within minutes the man had picked up the trail of the departing war party moving further west and reported his finding to the commander. Fairfax turned from the pathetic figure of a little girl. 'Might never know who these poor folk were,' he said grimly, 'but we haven't got time to make searches for identification.' His voice rose. 'Form a burial detail, sergeant. And make it quick. The Comanches ain't gone too far.'

He stepped round an overturned wagon and

walked towards the largest adobe which had the
words TRADING POST painted on the front. He
fingered bullet holes chipped in the white adobe
around the doorway before he entered. Inside it
was clear the contents had been plundered before
it had been fired.

'Look at this, sir,' Sinclair said as the captain
emerged again. The lieutenant was holding a
couple of broken whiskey bottles. 'The wagon here
must have been making a delivery. Looks like
whiskey was part of the consignment. You know,
we might have some drunken Comanches on our
hands.'

The two officers walked over to a heap of flesh
that had been a longhorn steer. Flies buzzed and
crawled over the gaping bloody hole where its
innards had been. 'I think we could be in luck,' the
captain said, turning away from the stench. 'It's
clear from the way the cattle have been hacked
that the varmints gorged themselves on the beef.
Probably first big meal they've had all season.
Huh, full stomachs, a crate or two of whiskey. I
figure the bucks have had themselves a party
someplace. Ain't gonna be in no prime condition
for scrapping.'

He walked over to where dirt was being
shovelled into the mass grave. He hurried the
men in their task and then took off his hat. He
said a few appropriate words over the mound and
looked at the climbing sun when he had finished.
'Mount up, men,' he said in a raised voice. 'We
ain't got time to lose.'

The war party proved easy to follow. Unexpec-
tedly, and fortunately for the Rangers, the

renegades had committed the sin of complacency. In the military manual, a cardinal sin, either because they were rusty after years of being spoon-fed on the reservation, or because many of them were young inexperienced bucks. Or, more probable, because they hadn't known the Rangers had been in the territory. Anyway, for whatever reason, the maverick Comanches hadn't posted sentries.

Captain Fairfax's scout had soon spotted them relaxing and carousing with the stolen whiskey in a ravine. A mile ahead of the ravine, Fairfax had grouped the command into three. After fixing noon for the attack, the captain headed one group straight ahead, to close in along the river. The remaining Rangers had been split into two semi-circular columns. One commanded by Lieutenant Sinclair to the east and the other under Sergeant Morley to the west, were to act as pincers.

As they neared the ravine they could hear voices. Sinclair and his men cut up swale and took position. The lieutenant looked at his watch and focused his eyes on the minute-hand approaching twelve. He indicated to his men the time was nearing. Across the void he could see Bill Morley's unit stringing out along the western ridge. The passage of time seemed interminable until, from Fairfax's lower position, a bugle pierced the noon air.

The Comanches, shaken from their complacency, sprang to arms under a crescendo of crackling Spencers. Some began to return fire while others grabbed at scattering mustangs and tried to ride out of the trap only to be met by Fairfax's disciplined Rangers. Some Indians kept low to the ground and began to worm their way upward but the brush that covered the slopes was no protection from the Rangers' repeating Spencers which took their toll from the ridge crests on both sides.

Sinclair's breech got hot in his hand. The sensation took him back to his old man's ranch years ago. They had herded some diseased beef into an arroyo and had slaughtered them in one long fusillade. Difference was, these weren't pitiful animals. They were well-armed men shooting back. He reminded himself of the mayhem the redmen had wrought on defenceless settlers; he thought of the little girl back at the trading post; and relentlessly worked his trigger finger.

After half an hour it was all over. Fairfax and Sinclair stood on a crest looking down at the carnage. With images of what the renegades had inflicted on civilians, the Rangers had given no quarter. There was not a breathing Indian left.

'They put up some fight, sir,' Sinclair was saying, 'despite the fact they hadn't been expecting an attack.'

'Yes, Lieutenant, we had the element of surprise. Wouldn't have been so easy in the old days. These renegades were a new generation, not brought up to fighting. They didn't know the old ways. Hot blood was all they got. Now for their pains their hot blood is spilled out all over the place. But, as you say, they put up a good scrap.'

The two men descended heavy-footed through

the scrub down the body-strewn slope. At the bottom Captain Fairfax called out to an old gnarled campaigner. 'What casualties, man?'

'Only three as I can make out, sir. One dead: Private Johnson. Young Wilson's caught one. Hand smashed. Then there's Sergeant Morley. He's in a bad way.'

'Bill?' Sinclair shouted. 'Where?'

'They're bringing him down, sir.' The old Ranger pointed across the river. 'Over yonder.'

Sinclair splashed through the shallow water. He made his way along the bank to where his non-com and old comrade had been lowered to the ground. The man was still, the side of his head sickeningly blooded. Janacek was trying to staunch the flow of blood from the head wound, while another Ranger was holding a canteen to the injured man's lips. But he was too far gone to take it. There was faint momentary recognition in his eyes when he saw Lieutenant Sinclair, then his head slumped.

Sinclair dropped to his officer's side. He eased open the man's tunic and probed for a heartbeat. He could feel nothing. No response, no movement. There would be no more jokes from the ugly son-of-a-bitch. 'Damn,' he breathed as he realized he was looking for a last time at his friend's face. He tried to close the still-open eyes, but couldn't.

The young Janacek broke down sobbing, the wet crimson rag still in his hand. Sinclair stood up. 'He's gone, sir,' he said quietly to the captain who was now at his side.

'I'm sorry, Lieutenant. I know you and he were close.'

'We started out as bunkmates. Joined up together; trained together.'

'Well, I knew him too. He was a good man.'

'The best, sir,' Sinclair croaked. He stepped into the river and stooped down to splash water over his face, mainly to hide his tears from his men. He wiped his face with his kerchief, and walked over to a prostrate Comanche. The dead man was clearly years younger than himself. 'Why, why?' he whispered. 'They had a decent life on the reservation.' Then his face hardened as he bent down and picked up the Indian's fallen weapon. He moved quickly to another corpse and picked up a further gun.

He inspected them then strode back to the captain with the brace of long-arms held out. 'Have you seen these, sir? New Winchesters. No wonder the civilians they attacked didn't stand any chance.'

The captain took one and inspected it. 'You're right, Lieutenant. Brand new. How the hell did Comanches get new weapons?' He scowled. 'Some critters have been gun-running.'

'What white men could do this?' Sinclair snapped. 'The bastards.'

'Some folks don't care how they make a dollar, Lieutenant.' He grunted a humourless, ironic chuckle. 'It's the American way. Free enterprise.' He looked closely at the weapon. 'I'll make a big issue out of this in my report. That's for sure.'

Resolution hardened in the lieutenant's eyes. 'Let me do some investigating, sir. In plain clothes. I owe that to Bill.'

'I know how you must feel, son. I'm an old

campaigner and over the years I've lost friends in combat. More than you'll ever know. But, as to you taking such action upon yourself, I can't allow that. It ain't up to us. We're Rangers, not federal agents. We do as we're ordered and make reports.'

There was no response in the lieutenant's features, so the captain continued. 'Rest assured, Lieutenant, there'll be an official enquiry once my report's in. I'll raise enough stink with the Adjutant General for that.'

'You know that'll take time, sir. Too much. By the time the administration back in Austin has debated and had their committee meetings, the trail will be colder 'n a lead-filled possum. Detail me to do some enquiring while the trail's hot. That's a special request, sir.'

'Don't ask the impossible, Lieutenant. You know I can't do that. Ain't our purview. We can only pursue a man if it is a task we are assigned to and there is a duly issued judge's warrant. And a judge can only sign a warrant if the criminal is named. Not knowing who's been doing the gun-running calls for detective work to which we ain't suited. It'll be up to the DA to employ detectives if he sees fit. He can use Pinkerton men. Local county officers will be circulated. That's the system.'

'This is personal, sir. I owe it to Bill.'

'That's another thing, Lieutenant. It's a bad Ranger that lets his personal feelings take over. Like it or lump it, we're servants of the public. That's the code we work by and that's why the Rangers were formed back in the '30s.'

He looked at his subordinate, noted the

agitation and frustration. He knew, for the moment at least, his official blatherings didn't amount to a hill of beans for the lieutenant. Then the old man's eyes softened. He gestured his head to take the lieutenant well beyond the earshot of any Rangers. 'Listen, son. You got a furlough due now this operation's over, ain't yuh?'

It took the lieutenant a second to bring his mind to bear on the captain's words. 'Yes, sir,' he replied, not seeing the relevance of the question to the conversation.

'Well, now, I can't be held responsible for what you do on your own time, can I, son?'

The look on Lieutenant Joel Sinclair's face changed.

ONE

It was early morning. The drovers had settled the herd for the night some miles out of Guadalajara so that the animals could graze and enter town the next day looking fresh. They could have got a higher price for the beef in Mexico City but that was another two hundred miles along the Santiago River and many of the critters wouldn't have made it. Most of the beasts were showing their ribs already, having being driven up from the Tierra Fria.

A domesticated strain of the *cimarrones*, the black, sharp-horned cattle were smaller than their Texas longhorn cousins. Although bred from the mustang cattle running wild in mesquite country, whatever wildness they had inherited had been eroded by the long trek to the Santiago. There were less than a hundred head of the critters and it didn't take long for the handful of *caballeros* to manoeuvre them into the pens on the outskirts of the adobe city.

As they'd approached the city Feliciano Chalco, the trail boss, had observed that the pens were already near full. That was bad news. It meant a glut and low prices for beef on the hoof. He kept his feelings to himself as he closed the last gate himself. Despite his being the head *honcho* of the outfit his attire was indistinguishable from that of the rest of his men. He wore working clothes of the same quality with the same conchos down his Sonora leggings and covered in the same trail dust. Out of necessity he ran his operation close to the bone, with barely enough riders to contain the herd.

'*Ole, mis camaradas,*' he said, turning to his men and histrionically raising his hands with clenched fists to indicate a long job completed. He pulled out a thin, unpretentious wallet and began to count the bills, then shrugged before he had finished and stuffed the meagre funds into his *segundo*'s hand. 'Hope there's enough there, Hernan,' he said, returning the empty wallet to his pocket. 'Get the boys some refreshment while I see what price I can negotiate. You've earned it. I'll see you in the usual place for the pay-off.' He waved a dismissing hand to his workers, and headed for the buyers' office.

The small group headed for the nearby *taberna* with, save for one, big-rowelled spurs jingling. The relief that comes with the end of a drive was apparent in the way they laughed and joked with one another, doffing their hats and slapping off the trail dust. Except for one they sported cartwheel sombreros. The odd man out was taller, blue-eyed and wore a stetson.

Inside the *taberna* Joe Branston exhibited a further difference from his *compadres*, taking lemonade instead of *tequila* or *pulque*. Booze had been one of his problems and it had been part of

his starting a new life in Mexico that he broke the
habit. Out of the six months he'd been in Mexico he
had ridden with the Chalco outfit for three. In his
time south of the Rio Grande he'd picked up a
modicum of Spanish and, despite his obvious Anglo
appearance, had been absorbed into the crew as
one of them.

After what seemed a lifetime of wandering
through the Mexican Sierra he'd fetched up at the
rancheria of Feliciano Chalco at round-up time.
The Americano being broke and despondent, it had
been a mutual coincidence of wants. In the wilder-
ness of the Tierra Fria, Chalco was short-handed
and cattle handling was the only trade Branston
knew. So the big man had joined the Mexican crew,
bringing in the critters, branding them and eventually riding swing on the drive to the Santiago
River.

While the Mexicans caroused in the smoky
atmosphere of the *taberna*, Branston smoked the
last of his cigarillos, joining in the *badinage* like a
native-born Hispanic. At last he looked at the clock
above the bar. Half an hour had passed and his
stomach was groaning in complaint at its empti-
ness. '*El patron* has taken a long time,' he said as
he worked the now-empty smokes-pack into a ball.
'He ain't vamoosed with the takings, has he?' he
added with a chuckle.

Carlos, his fellow swing rider, leaned over to
him. 'Do not say such things, even in jest. *Señor*
Chalco is the most honest *jefe* for whom I have ever
worked. He is respected by his men. You know
that. Should they hear you make such a suggestion, they might forget you are an *amigo,*

amigo.'

The American nodded and stood up. 'Only joshing, Carlos. Well, if you'll excuse me, boys, I'll take me a short stroll round the town; see the sights. See you later.' It was his first time in Guadalajara but he was no sightseer. The fact of the matter was that, remaining for so long in the *taberna* without booze and watching everybody drink like there'd been a drought, was becoming too much of a strain. Despite his will not to hit the bottle, even he had limits.

He bought a fresh pack of cigarillos at the bar and stepped outside to contemplate the scene dyed in bright colours by the high sun unfettered by cloud. He put a leathery hand inside his rough linen shirt and scratched, then shoved a cigarillo into the lips of the time-creased face. After lighting up he looked down the street in the direction of the beef commerce quarter. Registering no sign of *el patron* he moseyed along the thoroughfare.

Up a block, he moved through the market, casting an uninterested eye over the wares. Locals in ponchos and straw hats looked up at the stranger with reciprocated disinterest. Beyond the market he sensed the smell of food and his stomach groaned again. For use later he noted the location of the cantina from which the aroma emanated, then continued on his way, shortly passing the city's ancient cathedral but oblivious of its rich decorations. He terminated his mindless promenade outside the façade of the governor's palace, unaware that it was one of the finest examples of Spanish architecture in the

whole of Mexico. Such things were of little consequence to him: his mind was on other matters.

On his return, he fell in step alongside Chalco
who had completed his dealings and was heading
for the *taberna* to settle with his men. The trail
boss did not look the happiest of *hombres*, indicating recognition of his hired Americano with a
mere nod as they approached the building.

Branston liked the man. His roly-poly wife had
been friendly and his three shy black-eyed daugh-
ters respected by the men. His small ramshackle
hacienda and bunkhouse had been a haven for the
American during round-up with *Señora* Chalco
spoiling the crew with her cooking.

At the bar Branston steeled himself enough to
decline Chalco's offer of a drink. The boss took two
quick shots himself and walked over to where his
men were seated. Automatically a chair was
cleared for him. 'Times are bad, boys,' he said as he
sat down. 'We all knew we wouldn't be getting
top-dollar for the beef, but the bottom's clear dropped out of the cattle business, like everything else.
No dealer is interested in buying, save at give-
away prices.' He took out a bill-fold and counted
out each man's money in turn, sums agreed before
the start of the round-up but no bonuses.

'I know you were looking for continued employment,' he concluded after the money had been
dispensed, 'but the plain truth is I can't keep you
on, not even my regular hands.' Before returning
the thin amount that remained to his wallet he
studied it with a look that said, And what the hell
do I do with that?

The crew took the news quietly. They didn't need

their boss to tell them times were bad and the
casual hands, Branston amongst them, had all
been grateful to have found three months' work
with Chalco.

'What is all this glumness?' Hernan suddenly
said loudly. 'Times are not so bad we cannot drink
to the health of *el patron* and his honourable
family.' He stood up and returned from the bar a
minute later with two bottles of *tequila* which he
placed in the middle of the table for communal use.

They drank a toast to their former employer who
looked uncomfortable with the embarrassment of
their affection in the face of his inability to keep
them on. Then, 'What you gonna do now, boss?'
Hernan asked when all the glasses had been
refilled.

'Return home and weather the storm. Of course,
there'll be a job for any of you boys if things pick up
and I can restock. But it'll take a season or two the
way I see it.'

He stayed a short while longer talking with the
men then made his goodbyes with much hugging in
the Mexican way. Following his departure Branston stayed on lemonade but the *tequila* eventually
conjoined with the poor employment prospects to
take the heart out of the remaining Mexicans and
their depression began to show in an increasing
silence.

'Who's for eats?' Branston asked suddenly,
rising to his feet. 'I've spotted a *cantina* a short
ways along the street.'

'*Adelante*,' Hernan said, joining the American.
'Nothing like a full belly for putting the heart back
into a man.'

Two of their buddies agreed it was time to wrap themselves around some food and followed them to the door but the others were too interested in divesting themselves of their newly-acquired pesos on a liquid diet.

Once more outside, Branston pointed to the *cantina*. 'I'll see yuh in there. There's something I wanna get from my saddle-bag.'

At the tethering rail, his chestnut was glad to see its master, pushing its velvet muzzle into his hand when he got to its side and patted its neck. He opened the saddle-bags in turn and rummaged through the contents of each until he found a crumpled envelope crushed beneath the detritus. He smoothed it out to confirm it was what he sought. He pocketed it and made for the *cantina*.

'We ordered beans and tortillas all round, *señor*,' Carlos said as the American sat down beside them in anticipation.

'Anything that's quick getting itself on the table is OK by me, *compadre*,' Branston said savouring the aroma that infused the air.

Some time later he was pushing away an empty platter, having put away two helpings. He gave a grunt of satisfaction, took out a pack of cigarillos and dropped one by each of his *compadres'* plates. He flared a match and stretched his arm around the table to each man in turn. 'What are you *hombres* gonna do now?' he asked after they had all lit up.

'Who the hell knows?' the *segundo* said, exhaling smoke noisily. Bleary-eyed, he leaned towards the American. 'Our kind always get the ass end of the stick. Can't even scrape a living with moth-eaten cattle no more. You know, *señor*, I can't see our country ever getting on its feet. It has been looted and its wealth squandered by all and sundry.'

'That is true,' the one called Miguel agreed, in a drunken reflective tone. '*Caramba!* The devil and his son have taken a piece of our land. The southern provinces were gutted from us. The Americanos took Texas, California and New Mexico. We've been ripped apart by Spanish, French and British troops.'

'*Si*,' Hernan resumed. 'Now, thanks to the Spanish, we are a land of serfs, butchered by Apaches.' He looked around to check he wasn't overheard before adding, 'And ruled by a madman, General Diaz.' He quaffed some more tequila noisily. 'In my heart of hearts I do not know why a gringo such as yourself comes to a land such as this.'

Branston thought of the comrades he had seen die at his side during the war between the states not too many years ago; and of the newspaper reports he had caught of range wars and Indian fighting on the frontier. 'Believe me, *campañeros*, it ain't exactly a bed of roses north of the Rio Grande.'

Three heads nodded.

'What will Hoe do now?' Miguel asked.

Branston smiled. Despite his tutoring of them, their attempt to pronounce 'j' still came out as 'h' in the Spanish way. He had long given up trying to get them to say Joe properly.

He thrust work-hardened fingers into his vest pocket and withdrew the envelope he had extricated from his saddle-bag. He took out the letter and smoothed it as flat as he could on the table. 'Just remembered this. A letter from my kid brother Billy. Thought I'd look him up. Got a small spread in Texas handling horses last I heard. The Double B. Located near some place called Brightwater. If his business is on the right side of the balance sheet, mebbe he's got work for me.'

'You visited him before?'

'No.'

'How come you didn't pay him a call before setting out to look for work in Mexico?'

'Pride, something like that. It's a long story. The notion of sucking up to my kid brother stuck in my gullet for one thing.'

'That is understandable, *señor*. I too have a kid brother and know what a pain in the ass one can be. And now?'

'Hell,' Branston grunted. 'What's pride?' He jerked back a thumb towards the door. 'How much can you get fer pride in the market out there?' He looked back at the letter. His eyebrows rose and he moved his head back an inch or two as he sought to focus on the words. 'He's offering me a job here in the last letter that managed to track me down.' He peered at the date. 'Trouble is, it's a year old.'

'I do not want to put a wet blanket on the matter, *Señor* Hoe,' Miguel said, 'but his business circumstances may have changed in that time. It is a changeable world in which we live and times may be bad north of the Rio Grande.'

'Shut up,' Hernan said, ruffling the head of his

compadre. 'The *hombre* needs some hope, not your eternal pessimism. You go, Hoe. Whatever awaits you, things can't be as bad as down here.'

Branston nodded. 'Yeah, you're right. Ain't seen the kid for years anyways. Don't know what to expect. One thing though: he'll as-sure-as-hell have filled that vacancy by now. Leastways, I should be able to get a meal out of him. And we'll have a lot to talk about. That'll be good.'

TWO

The men rested their horses at Guadalajara then made the slow journey north to the Terra Fria and the small town where Miguel and Carlos lived, a spit and a hoot from the Chalco rancho. Hernan and Branston stayed over a night then headed north-east. It was largely unsettled country, hot and wind-blown. Vegetation and soil thinned out until there was little but the clatter of rock under their horses' hooves. They saw no one. The terrain was too bleak even for bandits. A rider survived on what he carried.

Beyond the arid plateau where Hernan's folks lived the locale became a little more hospitable. Just. Some soil, a hint of greenery.

When he was young Hernan senior, dispossessed like most Mexican peasantry, had taken his new bride up to the high country and had squatted on land nobody wanted. On terrain waterless and bleak they had survived, flourished and raised their family. Their means? The green cows that the old man still farmed.

Branston saw the serried ranks of the plants, like hands of tapered fingers grasping for the skies, before he saw the old folks' adobe tucked in beneath the crest of a ridge. The friend of the poor, the *vaca verde* or *agave*, is a God-given plant capable of supplying many of a human's needs: its thorns provide needles; its fibre is used for clothing and sandals; its tender inner spikes provide food; soap and medicine can be extracted from its roots, while its leaves provide roofing materials. But more important, the water-honey from its heart is the source of alcohol which fermented becomes the renowned *pulque*, *tequila* and *mescal*.

'Hernan,' the Mexican's father shouted, dropping a huge bundle of agave leaves from his back when he saw the dusty riders. After the embracing Hernan introduced the gringo. 'My house is yours, *señor*,' the old man said, pointing the way to the soddy cut into a slope.

Branston stayed over a couple of days helping the family in the harvesting then resumed his trek to the Rio Grande with the well-wishing of '*Esperanza*' in his ears. Travel was slow without a second horse but he made the border town of Del Rio without incident, rested up and headed out on the final lap to Brightwater.

It was four days later that he passed a cemetery on the top of a hill. He drew in and wiped his brow as he surveyed the markers. There were many graves. Most had wooden markers, some still upright, others angled and crumbling. A few had ornately carved headstones. Then there were a couple of elaborate stone plinths, decorated with angels. Even in death, men were not equal.

He waved to a couple of grave diggers finishing off a hole but they were too far away for him to speak and he didn't venture in. He didn't cotton to cemeteries. However the fading board over the graveyard entrance did interest him. The paint was peeling but the lettering was decipherable, labelling the sorry place as Brightwater Cemetery.

He looked down the trail and could see a settlement. That would be Brightwater. He warmed inside when he thought of Billy. What would he look like now? Boy, would they have things to talk about. He nudged his tired chestnut down the slope. 'Come on, pal, nearly there.'

As he neared the settlement he met a funeral procession travelling in the opposite direction. There was a simple box on the back of a buckboard, followed by a surrey and clutch of riders. You didn't need to be a man of letters to know it would be heading out to the last resting place back up the hill and the hole he had seen the old men preparing. He slowed his dusty chestnut and took off his trail-grimed hat in deference. Another lucky critter beyond the troubles of this world, he mused as the dour retinue continued past. For a moment he thought of another funeral, not too long ago, one which he had not attended. The funeral of a five-year-old boy. But he brushed it from his mind, settled his hat back on his head and nudged his horse towards a trough he'd spied on the edge of town.

Across the street a hand was tending a smoking stack of manure. Thankful that there was a slight breeze taking the pungent fumes in the opposite direction, Branston dropped from the saddle. While the animal was drinking, he cast his eyes up and down the street; stores, signs, a few folk going about their business. Brightwater was much as he expected it, no different from the other settlements through which he had ridden since he'd crossed the Rio Grande. When his mount had taken just enough to slake its thirst he gripped the bridle, overcame the resistance met in pulling back its head, and then led it to a rail shaded from the afternoon sun. After he had hitched it, he stepped up onto the boardwalk and made his way along main street.

Make for Brightwater, the letter had said. Then ask anyone there. My spread's just out of town. The Double B. Branston guessed it was named that way for Billy Branston. Hell, who knows, in the future it could stand for the Branston brothers.

Of the two brothers, the younger Billy had always been the go-getter, the one with ideas. Several times he had written Joe, inviting him out to join him. Got himself a little ranch, bronco-busting, horse breeding and trading. But Joe was too proud and hadn't taken too kindly to the notion. Very often, he didn't even reply to the letters. The Branstons had always been known for a streak of obstinacy and Joe had inherited more than his fair share. Furthermore, there had always been a hard chunk of envy with regard to his younger brother. Whatever the lad had put his hand to, he'd had a measure of success. The lucky son-of-a-bitch.

Of the two, Joe was the bum. He knew that. Never had what it takes in either the money or brains department to set up himself, always working for someone else for a pittance. Countless years of an unhappy marriage. Whose fault was that? His missus wanted the good things and said he had no ambition and could never get her the things she wanted. So, it was his fault. On the other hand, he thought she was a pain in the ass with her nagging. Like all these things, at the end of the day you can't point the finger of blame at any one thing or one person. He had enough brains to realize that. Anyways, whatever the reason, he spent increasing time with the booze and gambling while his missus occupied herself with the church. Then, a year ago, she ran away with one of the congregation. It had been inevitable. A guy from the choir with a high-pitched voice. Joe could smile at it now. But then....

He continued walking and appraising the place. Brightwater was a main town along that stretch of the Pecos and, in spite of its having been a port of call for every wagon train that had crossed the plain since the eighteenth century, the place was still small, its pathetic alleys snaking away from main street, its boardwalks rough and patterned with the tread of countless boots. A nowhere place you rode through and forgot.

He came to the town's one and only saloon. Over the batwings he squinted against the dim interior and could see a couple of guys seated at a table. A couple more at the bar. He gripped the top of the door in preparation to enter. He could ask directions in there. The ale and smoke smelled good. But he hesitated for a spell before letting go the doors, then walked past. He had seen a red

and white pole jutting out up the road a piece. A
barber's shop would be a sure place for getting the
information. And less of a temptation.

He walked further along the boardwalk, past a
store with toys in the window: dolls and wooden
soldiers. Paul had liked soldiers. When Joe's
missus had left she had taken him, their only son,
Paul. The little son-of-a-gun had only been five
years of age. Jeez, that really cut deep into his
spirit. Never saw the little fella again, except
when he looked into the bottle, which was
morning, noon and night. Lost his job. Had to
make do as a saloon-swamper, just pulling in
enough bucks to survive. Then the blow, like a
hammer-punch to the kidneys: news came young
Paul had died of diphtheria. That's when he really
hit the booze with a vengeance. As the months
passed the bottle rendered him unemployable.
From then on it had been odd jobs for cents. How
he'd managed to scrape enough together during
those dark days to keep his horse in feed he'd
never know.

It had been one night when he was thinking and
crying over Paul that he got a new perspective on
things. Where the notion came from he couldn't
say. Out of the blue he asked himself what would
Paul think of his pa today? Paul was now
changeless. The little fella would forever stay five
years old. But his pa was changing, even in the
short time since the infant's death, sliding further
into the depths. His love of uncorking a bottle was
rotting his character as well as his guts. It was in
that instant that he decided to kick the booze. But
he could only do it with a break of some kind. That

was when he'd saddled up the chestnut, uprooted his picket pin and had ridden south to Mexico.

That plan had been working well until *Señor* Chalco had laid the men off. The depths again, but he had been saved from going over the brink by remembering Billy and his invitation. In Guadalajara he'd dug out one of his brother's crumpled letters from his saddle-bag. It was a wonder he'd still got it. What the hell? He had no pride left. He'd drunk it all away. The answer was simple. He could make a new start working for his younger brother. God knows, the youngster had invited him often enough. Yes, new job, new town, new life. And no booze. Somebody Paul would be proud of again, just like he was when he used to toddle alongside his pa with his little fingers clutched round the man's hand.

He reached the barber shop. There were no customers and the barber looked up from his newspaper, happy to welcome a patron. When the man stood up Branston could see he was an Indian. Apache, he reckoned.

'Ain't never see'd an Injun barber afore,' Branston said as the man picked up a cotton sheet and flapped it in readiness, thinking the visitor was a customer. The action prodded Branston. Come to think of it, he could take a haircut and shave. Wouldn't come amiss, looking presentable when he met his younger brother again. He appraised the dark eyes and black hair. Then, 'How close to the scalp do you get?' he grinned as he settled into the chair.

'You know, mister,' the Indian said humourlessly as he fixed the sheet, 'I ain't ever heard that one afore. No, sir. No critter has ever talked about me scalping when I been a-barbering. That's a real new one, sir.'

Branston prised the sentence apart then guffawed noisily when he suddenly realized that the novelty of his question would not be in any way novel to the Indian.

'Figure you must hear that every day,' Branston conceded apologetically. The Indian grunted and after that they got on like a prairie fire. The trail-weary rider took a shave as well and when the barber had finished, Branston looked at the face in the mirror, checking that he hadn't been scalped. The puffiness and broken blood vessels of booze were evident, but at least the face was now clean and well-shaven. And he hadn't had a drink for more than six months to boot.

'Billy Branston,' he said, as he stood up and dropped coins into the barber's hand. 'You know where his spread is?'

'Billy Branston?' The Indian paused a second. 'Oh, you mean Billy Patch?'

It was Western custom for a town to tack a name to a man, suggested by some peculiarity. As a youngster his brother had lost his left eye and wore a black patch. Branston remembered and nodded. 'Yeah. Billy Patch. That would be him.'

'Sure,' the man said, pulled aside his apron to put the money in his pocket. 'Billy Patch's horse ranch. The Double B. Two miles east of town. Can't miss it. Turn north at the cedar slopes.' He flicked a brush over his customer's shoulders. 'You concerned with the estate or something?'

Branston looked puzzled as he pushed a finger

round the back of his collar to move itching hair bits. 'Estate? Don't know what you mean. No, I'm family. Billy's brother.' He chuckled. 'His long lost brother. Figure he's gonna be a mite surprised to clap his eyes on me again.'

'Gee, I'm sorry, Mr Branston.'

Branston grinned as he slicked his newly smartened hair before donning his hat. 'You don't have to apologize for asking, pardner.'

'No, sir. I was offering my condolences, not apologizing.'

His hat set square, Branston turned from the mirror. 'Condolences? What for?'

'You didn't know?'

'Know what, man?'

'This is awkward, sir.' The Indian hesitated in embarrassment. 'Well, I guess, you gotta learn from somebody. I'm afraid your brother met with an accident.' Further hesitation, then, 'A bad one.' Another pause. 'I'm sorry to say, he died as result.'

Branston's face blanched.

THREE

'That's why I didn't think you were kin,' the barber went on. 'Would have thought whatever family had turned up would have been at the funeral. They're holding it just about now. Saw it pass the window not too long back.'

Branston had dropped back into the barber's chair. 'I saw the cortège too.' His voice was becoming a low croak. 'Passed it as I rode in. Never figured....' He cradled his head in his hands.

'You want a drink or something, mister? I got some rye in my quarters. I can see you've had a shock.'

'Yeah. A stiff one if you've got it.' Then he remembered a promise he'd made to himself. 'On second thoughts, pal, no. Thanks for the offer.'

'You're welcome to sit down for a spell,' the redskin went on.

Branston shook his head. The barber gave him his hat and opened the door. His brain numbed, he stepped outside. The sky was grey and the whole town now had a bleak, cold appearance. With sickened stomach he mounted up and headed the chestnut out of town, retracing his way along the rising trail, this time none of the locale registering. He sickened further when he spied the fence marking the cemetery. There was the hearse that he'd seen earlier, a surrey and a clutch of horses. Two black-suited men were preparing to leave.

Heads looked up at the sound of hooves as he noisily drew rein at the low fence. He swung from the saddle and, without bothering to tether the animal, headed towards the departing mourners. Behind them the workmen he had seen earlier were topping up a grave with soil. The burial service was finished.

Branston came to a standstill, hat in hand, as the mourners advanced. A familiar emotion had come again into his life: grief. And he had missed yet a second funeral of a loved one. Paul, now Billy.

The first of the mourners, a tall man about Joe's age, replaced his stetson, disclosing as he did so the tattoo of a star on the back of his hand. The detail like the man himself went unnoticed. The remaining mourners neared and Branston put out his hand to attract the attention of the minister.

The man closed his Bible and moved out of line. 'You knew the bereaved?'

'Name's Branston, father. Joe Branston. Billy's brother.'

'I'm sorry you missed the service, Mr Branston.' The man was kindly-faced with understanding eyes. 'There was no one of the family here. But, as you can see, he was not without mourners. How far have you come?'

'Guadalajara.'

The grave-diggers had completed their task.
'Thank you, boys,' the priest said as they passed.
He turned back to Branston. 'Mexico? Some dis-
tance. You journeyed special?'

'No. Only just heard of his passing as I got into
town.'

'Oh, I'm sorry, son. This must have come as a
shock. My condolences.' He put out a colourless,
wizened hand. 'I am glad that you are with us.'

'Thanks, father.' He nodded his head backward.
'Who are the folks here?'

The minister indicated the three people who had
passed and were untethering their horses beyond
the fence. 'The fellow in the suit, that's Meadows,
the town lawyer. The other is the sheriff. The final
one I don't know. Maybe some acquaintance of your
brother.'

Over the minister's shoulder Branston could see
a young woman had stayed behind and was bend-
ing over placing flowers on the grave. 'And the
girl?'

'That's Miss Davis. Jenny Davis. A lady friend of
your late brother's, I believe.'

'Well, thank you for seeing to the necessaries,
father,' Branston said and he moved towards the
new mound of earth. By the time he got there the
woman had composed herself and was moving
away. He nodded to her as she passed him, then he
continued to the head of the grave. He ran the tips
of his fingers over the wooden marker bearing the
plain inscription: WILLIAM BRANSTON.

Oh Billy, he thought, you wrote me so many
times. I didn't even reply. If only I had have come
sooner. I've let you down in so many ways. There

were things to say. Now it's too late.

The newly dug soil was a darker hue than the surrounding earth. The difference would be temporary. The slight moisture in the disturbed soil would soon dissipate in the heat to blend it in with the rest. The flowers would quickly wilt in the sun and blow away. Then Billy's grave would be indistinguishable. The young man, just a memory.

He stood, hat in hand at the graveside. He stayed there for a long time with his thoughts.

When he made it back to town he booked in at a downtown drovers' lodge and settled his chestnut in the livery. He sat in his room until it was dark.

Then he went to the saloon and got drunk.

FOUR

Daylight was a bastard. It cut through the lace curtains and sliced his eyelids like some torture device out of Edgar Allan Poe. He had been too drunk to contemplate rational actions such as pulling drapes when he had staggered in and collapsed on the bed in the early hours. The sunlight was a double son-of-a-bitch, wrenching him back into an unhappy world.

He swung his legs round to get into a sitting position but the motion caused his head to spin and he nearly fell off the bed. Jeez. After a while he rose and staggered over to the dresser. He poured water into the basin and leant over the receptacle. It was cool and refreshing. There could be good things in life and dousing his face like this was one of them. He towelled himself and made his way downstairs.

The landlady went by the name of Else. Greying at the roots, her hair was dyed and frizzed. 'You're late, Mr Branston.' Her voice had that gravelly sound that came from forty years of smoking. 'But your tardiness is forgiven, seeing's you had a long ride in. Bacon, eggs?'

'Fine, ma'am,' he said, sitting at the table she

had indicated.

She looked at him through pebble glasses that reduced her eyes to such an extent Branston figured the only time he had seen orbs fixating him in the same manner was from a fishmonger's slab. Not an attractive sight, especially given the condition he was in.

'And coffee?' she went on, squinting the fish-eyes through the stinging smoke of the cigarette hanging from her browned lips.

'Fine, ma'am.'

'As black as it comes, I suppose,' she croaked, 'judging by the state you came in last night?'

'On the button, ma'am.'

He watched her walk to the kitchen. She had no behind and her body was as thin as a lath on a five-bar gate. She was perched on high heels like an emaciated vulture on a branch and when she walked it was with a mincing stagger, shoulders hunched in the manner of a bird of the same genus.

He closed his eyes trying to ignore the magnified clatter of her pottering about in the distant kitchen. 'That ought to bring you back to the land of the living,' she said when she returned minutes later with a cup of coffee.

Land of the living. It struck him as an appropriate figure of speech for someone returning from a funeral.

She watched him take a sip. 'I took you in last night out of benevolence,' she said as he replaced the cup in the saucer. 'But I assume you'll be moving on so I'd be grateful if you'd settle the bill expeditiously.'

He pulled his thoughts together to concentrate on her words. 'Of course, I'll pay whatever's necessary whenever you like, ma'am. But as to moving on, I ain't worked out any plans yet.'

She lit another cigarette and drilled him through the thick glasses. 'In that case, I'd be obliged if you'd find other accommodation. Your room will be needed for another guest who's arriving.'

'There are other rooms vacant, aren't there?'

'They've been booked in advance too.'

'Pity,' he said, taking another sip. 'You've got a swell place here.'

She nodded and tottered on the high shoes out of the room, leaving him to ponder. Why had she said she'd given him a room out of benevolence? The place was OK but it didn't look as though it was about to be inundated with visitors. He questioned her on it when she brought in his breakfast but she said she had nothing else to say on the matter.

Half an hour later, he was on the boardwalk with his warbag. He'd paid his bill and vacated the room. At least he'd got a couple of cups of coffee and a breakfast inside him, and his head was clearing. He slung his bag over his shoulder and headed down main street. He stopped at the building labelled Law Office. The name Tom Settle preceded the title of sheriff. He knocked and entered. There was an old guy seated at a desk working through some papers and a young beanpole of a fellow seated close by reading a newspaper.

'Sheriff Settle?' Branston asked.

The oldster at the desk looked up from his task. Despite his age the lawman had retained immaculately waved hair. His face was a contour map of red veins and he peered at his visitor through bushy white hairs that cascaded from his eyebrows. 'Yeah?'

'Name's Branston. Joe Branston. Came about my brother, Billy.'

'Oh, yeah. You were the guy who rode in after the funeral.'

'That's me. Had come visiting. Didn't know Billy had died and rode smack into his funeral. Hell of a shock. Anyways, heard tell he had an accident with a bronc and I was wondering if'n you could tell me what happened?'

The sheriff appraised him for a moment. 'Verdict at the inquest was accidental death. Plain and simple.'

'Well, as his brother, I'd like to know a little more.'

'You could see the doc. He should be able to give you more details.'

'Of course. Where might I find him?'

The younger man had folded his newspaper and had been listening to the conversation. 'His surgery is down the street a spell,' he said. 'Fred Adams. You can't miss it.'

Branston moved back to the door, his hand reaching out for the handle. 'You knew Billy?'

The lawman ignored the question causing his visitor to pause without opening the door. 'Listen,' Settle said, breaking the awkward silence. 'What happened, happened. It was for the best. I don't see the need to talk about it. Like I said, you have a word with the doc if you want the medical side.'

Branston was puzzled. 'I don't understand, Sheriff. It was for the best? That's a mighty odd thing to say in the circumstances.'

'Mr Branston, it's best you conclude your affairs here and return wherever you came from.'

The sheriff was sounding like the landlady at the drovers' lodge. Branston suddenly felt like he'd got the plague or something. 'I don't get your drift, Sheriff.'

'Listen. Your brother's death will be upsetting enough for you. Christ, I understand that. Just, ain't no need for you to get more upset.'

Branston's hand fell from the door handle and he stepped back. 'Upset about what? What should make me more upset?'

The sheriff sighed. 'Look, Branston. The long and the short of it was your brother was just about to be arrested. The accident he had saved everybody a lot of trouble.'

Branston's face hardened. 'That's a mighty harsh thing to say to a man who's just lost kin.'

'Yeah, I'm sorry. I told you I didn't want to say more. You pressed me to say it.'

'I think you've got to say something,' Branston said, squaring up to the desk. 'In fact, I ain't leaving until you've told me what needs to be said. Why were you going to arrest him?'

The sheriff sighed. 'OK. It's like this. A bunch of Comanches broke out the reservation up in Indian Territory. Turned wild and did a lot of killing before they was stopped by the Rangers. Anyways, turns out somebody had supplied them with new repeaters. Without the new weapons they couldn't have done the damage they did. Took me some time but I eventually found out it was your brother doing the gun-running.'

'Billy?' Branston dropped into a wicker chair. 'I don't believe it. Gun-running? Causing people to die? You got it wrong, Sheriff.'

The lawman grunted. 'How well did you know your brother? How long is it since you knew him?'

'Ain't see'd him in some ten years now.'

'That's a long time, Branston. A guy can change. Or reveal a hidden side to his nature. It's clear from the way you're talking, there was a side to him you didn't know.'

Branston shook his head. 'I ain't persuaded.'

'The evidence was building up against him,' the younger lawman put in. 'We'd got some leads but it was clinched after the accident at his ranch. That was when I found a couple of repeaters on the property that came from the same batch used by the Injuns.'

'Circumstantial evidence! The guns could have been planted by someone wanting to incriminate him. Those ain't reasons to hang a man. What kind of law you got around here?'

'What we've told you was the tip of the iceberg,' Settle continued. 'There was other evidence. Listen, it wasn't just us that was after him. The DA in Austin had a file on your brother an inch thick. I was liaising with the authorities. They'd told me to keep him under surveillance until a state marshal came in to make the arrest. In the meantime they'd given me instructions to arrest him if he looked as if he was making a break for it.'

Branston stared at the floor shaking his still-fuzzy head. This was all too much to take in.

'Meanwhile,' the sheriff went on, 'rumours were spreading round town and things were hotting up. A real awkward situation was developing. There's a lot of folk here lost kin and friends to the Comanche renegades. This is a small town and rumours spread fast. Somehow folks had got wind that your brother was responsible for supplying the guns. I was dreading him doing anything stupid before the DA's man came. I tell you, I would have had a hell of a lotta trouble trying to stop somebody lynching him once I'd got him into custody.'

Branston's head still moved in disbelief as the lawman continued. 'I have to tell you, for what your brother caused I despised him. But, much as I hated him, it would have been my job to have stopped them noosing him to the nearest tree. I could forsee all that so I'd made arrangements to get him outta town quick if it fell that I had to make the arrest. We wus planning to get him to Austin after I'd made the arrest. You ask Lenny, my deputy, here.'

The beanpole nodded. 'True.'

'Anyways,' the old man went on, 'that's about the size of it. Next thing we knew, he'd been thrown from a horse. Fell bad, turned out fatal. I'm telling you, he'd have been hanged for sure. Gun-running is a capital offence. He knew that. Ain't a pleasing thing to tell kin such as yourself but, like I said afore, the accident saved everybody a heap of trouble, your brother included.'

After a long silence, Branston raised his head

from his hands. 'Sheriff, this smells. I'm gonna ask some more questions.' He rose and returned to the door. 'Frank Adams, the name of the doctor, you say?'

The lawman nodded as Branston turned the handle. 'Listen, I'm real sorry you had to find out this way,' he added; but Branston had gone before he'd completed the sentence.

FIVE

Slowly he made his way down the street, pondering on how his ramshackle existence had again been disturbed. He had come to Brightwater in the hope that his life would take a new turning. It had, but not in the direction he had expected. He thought on what the sheriff had said and it gave meaning to the way the townsfolk looked at him as he moved amongst them on the boardwalk. The cold looks of people who didn't know him and did know him at the same time. It was a small town and news soon spread.

Eventually he came to the sign F. ADAMS MD and he knocked at the door. While he waited he turned his back and surveyed the street which is why he didn't see the face appear at the window. Furtive eyes appraised him and the face withdrew. After a second fruitless knock he tried the handle but the door was locked. The doc was probably out on calls, was his conclusion. Temporarily thwarted, he wondered who else might be able to enlighten him. Who else beside the law and the medical profession were concerned with a death? The coroner, that was who. He made enquiries of a passerby and got directions to the end of the block.

Elmer Springer doubled up as coroner and undertaker. His place smelled funny and was dark inside on account of the windows being painted red. Springer himself would not be mistaken for a coroner or an undertaker, barely thirty with a close-cropped ginger moustache and dressed more akin to a puncher than a government official. Nevertheless, although in appearance he was not what Branston had expected, he still had the parsimonious manner that went with the office. As he learned his visitor's identity and the nature of his enquiry he pulled quietly at his moustache,. then flicked through a file. He pulled out the death certificate bearing the name of Branston's brother and stating 'accidental death', pure and simple.

His conversation consisted of terse yeses and noes until Branston expressed some disquiet at the verdict. 'Nothing nobody has told me so far,' Branston said, 'explains how an expert horseman falls off a horse and gets himself killed.'

'You'll have to face facts, Mr Branston,' Springer said. 'Accidents do happen. Even when a man knows what he's doing. You want to know the exact medical circumstances, see Doc Adams. Now if you'll excuse me, I have work to do.'

'I've tried but can't get no reply from his door.'

'This might be a small town, Mr Branston, but we are all busy at one time or another.'

'Obliged for your time, Mr Springer,' Branston said, realizing he would get no more from the official. 'Good day.'

Like everyone else Branston had an important task. His was to wash away his problems. Once again he joined the ranchers and barflies in the saloon. He'd downed his second drink and was about to reorder when an oldster appeared from nowhere. 'So there you are, Mr Branston.' The man was in shirt sleeves, red patterned suspenders pulling on high-waisted pants.

'You have the advantage, mister,' Branston said, pushing his tin mug across the counter for a refill.

'The name's Meadows. Anthony Meadows. Your late brother's lawyer. We need to have words, Mr Branston. Business.'

Branston turned from his important task and appraised the man. 'So, Mr Meadows. What can I do for you?'

'It's more the other way round, sir. Could you postpone your drink until we've had a talk? Preferably in my office. It's across the street.'

Branston examined the diminishing stock of coins in his hand, then thrust them back into his pocket. 'Couldn't stay here too long anyhow.'

'The long and the short of it is,' Meadows was saying, minutes later in his office, 'you inherit your brother's estate. Mainly the ranch, of course. There'll be no probate trouble on that score, as far as I can see.'

Branston mussed his face with his hand. 'You know, I hadn't thought of any of those things.'

'However,' Meadows went on, 'your brother's bank account has been frozen. So you'll not be able to claim any liquid assets. They have been sequestered by the authorities.'

'How's that?'

'All monies will be deemed to be the result of

illegal transactions with the Indians. You've seen the sheriff, so you'll know about that.'

'Yes. He told me about the charges he was putting together.'

'Well, the selling of arms to redskins is against state and federal law.'

'The charge ain't proven,' Branston snapped. 'There's been no trial. Billy's innocent anyhows.'

'How do you know?'

'I just know.'

'When you spoke with the sheriff and coroner, did you voice your misgivings to them?'

'Only to the sheriff.'

'You need to guard what you say to folks, Mr Branston. It's the easiest thing in the world for a stranger in a strange town to get off on the wrong foot.'

If the suggestion was heard it was not acknowledged.

'Heed my advice, Mr Branston,' the lawyer went on. 'Take the ranch, sell up and leave town. Believe me, you will only be drumming up animosity towards yourself if you persist with any matter contrary to the legal view.' He looked at the clock on the wall. 'Look, I have some time in hand. Come and have a look at the ranch.'

'Hell, why not?'

Meadows stood up and collected his jacket from the stand near the door. 'We'll take my gig. It ain't far but I figure your hoss'll be stove up after your long journey out here.'

Half an hour later they were seated in the gig atop a ridge looking down into a small valley. There were a couple of shacks surrounded by a network of corrals and, at the back, a stretch of pasture enclosed by a barricade of cottonwood logs. Half a dozen horses grazed. 'Not exactly big,' Meadows said. 'Five hundred acres according to the deed.'

'Did Billy have anyone working for him?' Branston asked when the gig had been halted outside the main cabin.

'Not many permanent as I can make out. I wasn't conversant with the details of his operation. Took men on as casual hands when he needed them, as far as I know. Hiring and firing with changes in the work load, that's normal in ranching.'

'Don't I know it,' Branston grunted. 'But Billy must have had some regulars. You can't work a spread, even a small one, without some back-up that knows their way around.'

'Now you come to mention it, there was a youngster hanging around. Saw him at your brother's side when he came into town from time to time. Some greenhorn that your brother had picked up north someplace and was training up. What was the fellow's name? Dave, that was it. Dave Harleyson as I recall. Something like that. Then, of course, there was Clem and Luke. But they were more buddies of Billy's than work hands. They might have helped on the ranch but they didn't look like wranglers to me the few times I saw them. I don't know. They weren't around much anyhow. Good job too. Didn't like either of them.'

Branston scanned the buildings. There was no sign of current habitation.

'Where are they now?'

'Disappeared; all three, so I hear.'

They alighted from the gig and mounted the veranda. Meadows turned the key in the lock and pushed open the door of the main cabin. Branston accepted his invitation and entered. Of the two brothers Billy had been the dude and, even out here in the wilds, it showed. The conditions were humble: crude clay floor, mud chimney, rough beamed ceiling; But there was class in the furniture and the dwelling's accoutrements, a centre-piece being a polished teak table with brass candelabra.

Branston drew his finger across the table's surface and examined the dust on his fingertip, then looked around the undisturbed room. 'Reckon this stuff won't stay here once it gets around that the place is vacant. If nothing else, a body could make a few dollars out of the contents. The sooner I move in the better.'

Outside Branston vaulted the cottonwood barricade and approached the horses. They glanced up at the newcomer, then returned to their grazing. He patted the flank of the nearest. The animal raised its head and Branston stroked its muzzle. 'If only you could talk, fella.'

He inspected the troughs. They needed topping up so he found a pail and, with Meadows watching, worked at the pump until he'd got a flow going.

'How much stock is there?'

'What you see here,' Meadows said as water gushed into a pail. 'There's a small herd up on the western pasture. Mebbe twenty head.'

'I'd like to check 'em out.'

'There'll be plenty enough time for that.' Meadows breathed deep, like he didn't cotton to the way the conversation was going. 'See here, Branston, I may as well be blunt. My sincerest advice is to sell up. There are too many people with a grievance against the Branston name for life to be comfortable for you around here. Look at it this way: you capitalize on the property and you'll be going out of town with more than you came in with. Better'n a kick up the ass. Or worse.'

'I'm staying,' Branston said, picking up the pail and walking towards to the trough. 'At least until I've cleared up whatever's going on here.'

Meadows accompanied him. 'What do you think has been going on here?'

'For a start, Billy had a talent for riding ever since he was a kid. Natural flair. I'm told he was killed by a horse fall and it don't set right with me that he just fell from his saddle.' He upturned the pail into the trough. 'Mebbe my brother was murdered and his death made to look like an accident. Anybody think of that?'

Meadows paused. 'No, don't reckon anybody did.' Then the lawyer shook his head. 'Mr Branston, things really are as simple as they look.'

'What's more,' Branston went on, ignoring the comment and heading back to the pump, 'with regard to these charges the sheriff is mumbling about, I reckon my brother was set up. Framed. Wouldn't be the first time it's happened in the world. So I'm going to clear his name. The family name. I can't leave town without doing that.'

'I see that trail as the trail towards big trouble.

Trouble you can do without.'

Branston looked around the spread. 'Hosses have enough water and pasture for a spell. Let's lock up and get back to town.'

They didn't speak much on the return journey. Back in Meadows' office the deeds were duly transferred to Branston. 'As I said,' the lawyer concluded, adding the final signature and handing the document over, 'your brother's bank account has been sequestered. How are you fixed for cash?'

Branston shrugged his shoulders. 'What you see is what I got.'

'All the more reason to sell up and get out. But at least there are no debts on the property.'

Branston pocketed the deeds, stood up and moved to the door. 'We're talking about dignity and respect here, Mr Meadows. Not material things. I'm sticking around for a spell.' He patted the deeds in his breast pocket. 'Leastways, I got a place to lay my head.'

'For a night or two, mebbe, but a place needs money to run. Not only living expenses but other expenditures. Local taxes, for instance.' He nodded to the world outside the window near his desk. 'I've told you how the Branston name stands in these parts. From what I gather from the scuttle-butt, no suppliers will give you credit. And you won't get a red cent out of the bank.'

'I didn't say nothing about trying to run Billy's spread. I don't know what my plans will be in that direction. I know beef but not horses. But I'll tell yuh one thing, I am staying long enough to find out a few things.'

'Listen, Branston, there are two frontiers: the one that folk read about in dime novels and the real one. You've been reading too many books. This stuff about murder and framing, riding out here and clearing his name: that's straight out of one of them fanciful stories.'

The lawyer leaned to his side and cleared away some of the grime from the window pane. 'Look out the window here.' He nodded to the street. 'What do you see? Tradefolk. Punchers. Ordinary folk. They live ordinary lives. Their main concern is making a living. For most it means barely scratching an existence. You know, the puncher is the most exploited worker in the country? Works for a pittance. A few dollars and found. None of them fancy trade unions like you got in the cities. OK, on account of life being hard living off nature, sometimes you get crooks, like anywheres else. I'm afraid you'll have to face it, your brother was one who couldn't make it along the straight and narrow. And, one way or another, he has paid the price. No, it ain't all rootin'-shootin' out here like city folk think. Real makes me smile, some of the things I read in them smart novels.'

'Wouldn't know about all that,' Branston said, opening the door. 'Don't read much.'

SIX

Outside he checked his funds. Not quite zilch, but in terms of trying to run a business like a horse ranch, just shy of having to beg on a street corner. Never mind a horse ranch, being kicked out of the drovers lodge meant the priority for his grubstake had to be feeding himself. He made his way to the General Store and provisioned himself with coffee and a clutch of canned food. He was just picking up the change when another customer entered.

The man had short, stumpy legs and wide hips with the consequence that he trudged flat-footedly rather than walked. 'Hi, Jake,' the newcomer said.

'Afternoon, Cole. And what can I do for you?'

The man called Cole delayed replying but looked Branston up and down as he gathered his purchases. He waited until Branston was heading for the door and then said in a loud voice, 'You know who that bozo is? Billy Patch's brother. Another Branston.'

'The hell it is,' the proprietor mouthed. 'And I just served the critter!' His voice rose. 'You, mister. Don't come in here again. I ain't trading with the likes of you or your kind.'

Branston paused in the doorway. 'A real Brightwater welcome. I ain't guessing why. Thanks, neighbours.'

He loaded up his saddle-bags and took a steady ride north. Back at Billy's ranch he set his chestnut loose in the corral and fed him a measure of oats. Horses in the other corrals ambled across and peered curiously over the rails at their new owner.

'Which of you bastards killed my brother?' he asked. There was mutual appraisal for a spell, before he concluded, 'Whichever one of you it was, you didn't mean it. That is, if it was one of you and not some two-legged critter.'

He moved to a smaller enclosure containing a single horse. As he touched the fence, the animal charged at him, then halted a few paces away to stomp its defiance. 'Reckon you were Billy's prime stud, weren't you, fella?' Branston said, assessing the features of the creature. The horse was tall with a deep chest indicative of strength and stamina. After a spell its demeanour changed and it ambled over towards him on long legs. Warily Branston put out his hand. Then it butted a velvet nose against his outstretched palm. He stroked it along the jaw-line, noting the fine-boned head. He was no horse-rancher but he figured there was some Arab in its pedigree.

The animal jerked, backed and began its aggressive stomping. Branston smiled. 'You're showing me you got spirit, ain't yuh, fella? But you ain't fooling me completely. There's some friendliness there, dying to come out.' He returned to the first corral and noted that it backed off to a stable. He clambered over the fence and heard the snicker of horses as he approached. Inside the stable he found a couple of mares in stalls. Grinning at their friendly inquisitiveness, he checked their water. After he'd freshened it up he replenished their oat troughs.

It was still light when he'd finished so he found a saddle-broke horse, cinched him up and rode out to the far pasture to investigate the rest of the herd that Meadows had spoken about. As he neared, he could see why Billy had opted for the site. There was ample grass, trees for shade, with a creek cutting through it. The natural resources would not be enough for a spread-owner with big ambitions but sufficient to support a small herd.

As he approached he could see the animals grazing. He reined in, not wishing to spook them and shaded his eyes to study them from afar. It didn't take him long to make out a stallion, proud and clean-lined, maybe two years at the most. With a dozen mares to protect, along with their colts and yearlings, the male was picking his way stiffly through the throng, the erect head indicating he was well aware of the interloper while the purposefulness and direction of his gait bore witness to his being prepared to defend his herd.

Leaning on his saddle horn, Branston nodded in satisfaction. Reckon Billy knew what he was doing, he thought. Along with the Arab back at the ranch and the stallion here he'd got himself a couple of good studs. Between the two there was potential for developing good stock with a classy strain.

He turned in the saddle and took in the physical aspects. For the most part, the terrain had natural boundaries of rock and, where there were possible exit routes, rough timber fencing was in place.

'Billy sure worked hard fixing this up,' he said to himself.

It was dark when he got back to the ranch. He lit up some oil lamps and located a tub in the bunkhouse where Billy had had the skill and energy to fix a pump. After a good soak he heated some beans, took coffee and hit the sack.

SEVEN

Branston hadn't been waiting long outside the school before the door burst open and a flood of raucous kids cascaded into the yard. Meadows had told him that the young woman at the funeral had been the local schoolteacher. In amusement he watched the children disperse to the four points of the compass, chattering, laughing, then he crossed the dusty playing space. He mounted the wooden steps and knocked the open door as he entered.

It was a one-room shack and the teacher was tidying away books in the all-purpose classroom. She looked up from her task. Not with the hard patrician look that he remembered from the old bat of a school-ma'am from his own learning days. This was a mere girl with porcelain skin and hair a lustrous coil of ash-gold. A real honey. It didn't have to be chalked in big letters on a blackboard to recognize what Billy had seen in her. 'Yes?' The voice matched the softness of her appearance.

'Miss Davis?'

'Yes.'

'Joe Branston, ma'am,' he said, doffing his hat. 'Billy's brother.'

There was a pause, then, 'Oh'. Although only one syllable, the sound was laden with emotion in response to the name.

'His lawyer, Mr Meadows, he told me I could find you here.'

The young girl composed herself and laid down her armful of books to move around the desk and shake his hand. 'In circumstances other than the one that brought you to town I would say I was glad to meet you, Mr Branston.'

'It wasn't Billy's passing that brung me. I only learned of that since I've arrived.'

'Whenever you learned, it must have come as quite a shock. I'm sorry, Mr Branston.'

He nodded. 'Thanks.' He breathed deeply. 'Anyways, I'm glad to meet you too, ma'am.' He looked around the room: the flag hanging limp by the blackboard, a large-lettered alphabet on the wall, and all over the place funny pictures the way kids draw. Huh, he hadn't been in a classroom since a child himself. There was a smell, maybe chalk or something like that, that tightened up his guts reminding him when he first entered a classroom as a terrified child with his best trousers on and hair slicked down with butter. 'I was wondering,' he went on, 'if'n we could talk a spell? When it's convenient.'

'Of course. I'd like that.' She stepped back and appraised him. 'Yes. I can see your brother in your eyes.' She smiled. 'That wistfulness. And the hesitancy in the mouth.' She chuckled sadly with a recalled pleasure. 'The same little-boy mother-me look.'

He shifted in embarrassment as she made a

circuit around the little desks picking up pencils and crayons. 'You saw my little charges?'

He looked puzzled.

'The children.'

'Yes,' he grinned. 'Rather face a herd of longhorns than take them on. Don't know how you handle so many.'

'Oh, I normally have far more than that. School is purely voluntary in the county and it's harvest time so many of my charges are helping in the fields. Won't see them again until next fall.' She laughed. 'By which time the little darlings will have forgotten everything I've taught them.'

'You do yourself an injustice, ma'am. With such a teacher, I'm sure some sticks.'

She finished her task of tidying up and glanced around the room. 'Listen, it's not very amenable here. Shall we go back to my place? It's not far. I usually take a pot of tea at this time. After talking all day, I surely need it.'

'That'd suit me fine, ma'am.'

'The name's Jennifer. Jenny to my friends. Billy called me Jenny. I'd prefer that over ma'am. You no doubt realize that being called ma'am is a hazard of my profession.'

'Ain't hard to figure.'

'Well, Jenny it is to be,' she said, closing a cupboard door and glancing around the room in a last check.

'In that case, I'm Joe, not Mr Branston.'

Jenny's house was a magnificent two-storey building on the edge of town.

'Don't think this comes out of a teacher's salary,'

she smiled, noting his wide-eyed look as she opened the gate in the white-painted fence. 'My father was the local judge. Ma had died when I was young and when he finally passed away, some three years ago now, he left the place to me. Left me some money too. Something to draw on to keep the place running.'

He followed up the path edged by flowers. She fingered the petals cascading from a hanging basket of flowers fixed to the porch roof. 'Otherwise I would have had to have sold up a long time ago,' she went on putting a key in the door. 'Replacing shingles, painting, these things cost a fortune these days. Billy helped, of course, but he led a busy life, having the ranch to run and all.'

Branston took off his hat as he followed her inside. Like the outside, the interior was kept trim with the touch of a woman, ornaments and antimacassars on the chairs. 'Now you settle yourself down while I put on the kettle,' she said, disappearing towards the kitchen.

Over tea they talked of Billy and exchanged potted life stories. Then Branston asked, 'What's your opinion about this allegation of him gun-running?'

'I loved your brother, Joe. But he was a complicated man.'

Disappointment distorted his features. 'You mean you believe the tale?'

'What I'm saying is that I don't know what to believe. And much of his time was unaccounted for.'

'For Lord's sake, he was running a business.

That would occupy him, just like your job takes up much of your time.' He drained his cup and returned it with some finality to its saucer. 'Anyways, I don't believe it.'

She looked at the grandfather clock. 'It's getting late. I need to get started on the cooking. You'll share a meal with me?'

'It ain't my way to impose, ma'am.' He reached for his hat. 'Much obliged for your hospitality and mighty glad to have made your acquaintance.'

She stayed his hand with hers. 'Listen, Joe, we've just met. I can tell by the way you're calling me ma'am again that you're unhappy about our conversation. You think my doubts display disloyalty to your brother. I loved Billy and if he were alive today I'd stand by him through thick and thin. But that doesn't mean I didn't recognize he had failings. I have failings. We all do. Love and loyalty don't affect the truth. You've been around long enough to know that.'

She clenched his hand and he could see gathering moisture in her eyes. 'Listen,' she went on, 'you and I, we shared Billy. That makes us kind of family together. Your having a meal under my roof is not a matter of imposing. I'd dearly like you to stay. We can talk some more. You can give me that, can't you?'

He coughed in embarrassment. 'I'd better be going, ma'am.' He cleared his throat again and added, 'I mean Jenny.'

She chuckled. 'And you can be a stubborn mule too. Just like your brother. Listen, you ornery pepperpot, have a smoke or something while I get busy in the kitchen. You like range steak?'

Slowly his hand withdrew from his hat.

'Tell me about him when he was young.' It was
dark outside and she was talking to him across
the candles flickering in the middle of the table. 'I
would have liked to have known him then.'

He finished chewing on some meat and took a
sip of wine. 'His youth was my youth. We spent a
lot of time together. Funny how, when you think
back to being a kid, it was always sunny. We had
our ups and downs, a few childish arguments, but
we were buddies. I think it was because we didn't
compete with each other like other brothers seem
to do. Don't know why. We just had this thing
going between us. Huh, me always getting him
outa scrapes.'

'Your father died when you were young, didn't
he? Maybe that would have cemented your
relationship with Billy.'

'Maybe. I was only a young pipsqueak myself
but, as the elder, I saw myself as the man of the
family. Billy just accepted it, I suppose.'

Jenny dabbed her mouth with a napkin. 'What
was he like? Really like.'

'I don't know what you want to hear. You and
me, we got different viewpoints. He was my kid
brother is all. Had an obstinate streak in him, I'll
tell you that. Always did, the little varmint.'
Prompted by talk, memories came flooding back.
'Huh, always got his own way of doing things, too.
Tell him to do something, he'd nod his head. And
when you came back he'd done it different. Gee, he
sure screwed up a lotta things that way. Wouldn't
be told. Huh, the things he bust.'

'What about girls?'

He smiled. 'Funny thing, that was. He was younger'n me, but he was chasing after females long before I was. Billy matured a lot quicker in those affairs, I figure. Or maybe I was just more occupied with chores and helping Ma. Yeah, he was different to me in that respect. And not so shy as me neither.'

'Was he serious about any of them?'

'Huh, you knew him. Was he serious about anything?'

'We were serious.'

'You must have been something special to have had that effect on him.'

'You haven't answered my question.'

He pondered on it. 'No, can't say I ever recall a girl he was serious with.' He paused, looked at her. 'You are something special.'

She looked down at her meal. 'How'd he lose his eye?'

'Did you ask him?'

'Yes. A childhood accident is all I could get out of him.'

Branston's face changed, like something was welling up and he was trying to hold it back. 'The son of a gun!' It was some time before he spoke again. 'It was me. Fooling around with a slingshot. You know, the way kids do. I must have been around twelve. That'd make him nine. Nasty business. Lot of blood. Jeez, we had to get him to the doc fast. But there was nothing the doc could do, apart from take it out.' He paused. 'And he didn't tell you I was the cause of his injury?' He shook his head. 'The son of a gun.'

He wiped his hand across his face as though to wipe away the flush that had come to it. 'Yes. I was the reason why my kid brother looked at the world with one eye. Huh, the name Billy Patch came pretty quick from the kids at school. In a way he seemed to enjoy it. You know, like a guy wears a tattoo or an Indian buck carries battle scars. Young Billy, he always liked to be different. Hell, some way to be different. Mind, he had the edge on the other kids when it came to playing pirates!'

He sighed. 'Causing somebody permanent damage, you carry it around the rest of your life. You know that? Makes me cringe every time I think on it. A moment's thoughtlessness and.... Yet he never held it against me. Can't remember even one time when he blamed me for it, or even mentioned it. He could have done, when we were arguing. If he had have done, I wouldn't have had an answer. I owe him for that.' He finished another mouthful. 'The little sod-buster would have been real handsome hadn't have been for that.'

Jenny smiled through the candle-light. 'He was handsome enough for me.'

Branston nodded to his cleaned plate. 'Well, Jenny, that was a swell meal. You must let me help with the dishes before I go.'

'No. You're my guest.'

'I insist. I ain't good at many things in this life but I can dry dishes.'

'Well, at least let your dinner go down. Light up your pipe again. I like the smell of tobacco around the house. Reminds me of Billy.'

'He smoked a pipe?' Branston asked incredulously.

She laughed at the mental image of baby-faced Billy with a pipe clenched between his teeth. 'No. But he was never without the makings.'

Branston took out his worn pouch and refilled his pipe. 'I ain't yet sold on the story about Billy's accident,' he said after he had lit it from the candle. 'The lad was a good horseman.'

Jenny looked puzzled. 'You're the first to question it.'

'Was anybody after him? I mean, had he crossed anybody that might hold a grudge against him?'

'Not that I know of.'

Branston stood up and investigated an engraving of whalers on the wall. 'What about his buddies?'

'I didn't like them, I'll say that. Shady types.'

'Meadows told me about those. Forgotten their names now.'

'Clem and Luke. Whenever he was late in meeting me, it was usually them he'd been drinking with. He went away with them a lot too.'

'Where to? Doing what?'

'Don't know. He had his hidden side. That's why I'm not so quick to question as you. But I know one thing, if Billy had been in any trouble like folk were saying, it's my opinion they would have been behind it.'

'I'll put them on my list of folk to check out.' He sat down again and watched smoke curl to the ceiling. 'Had anything happened, previous to what folks are calling an accident? Anything out of the ordinary?'

'Now come to mention it it did strike me he was getting jumpy over something.'

'What about?'

'Don't know.'

'Well, that's something else to work on.'

'You think he was deliberately killed?'

'I ain't ruling out the possibility. Something doesn't sit too right in this business. I've got investigating to do. But it's gonna have to be on my own 'cos the sheriff don't seem interested. The whole thing's a closed book to him.'

'Listen, if there's anything I can do to help, let me know.'

'Thanks, Jenny.'

EIGHT

Branston sat on the boardwalk, took off his hat, mussed his face and watched the comings and goings of townsfolk.

He'd ridden into town early that morning to try to find out more about Billy's three associates. He'd approached storekeepers and passers-by with his questions about them. If he hadn't already realized that word had got round town who he was, he knew now: the original stares of curiosity had become looks of disdain. The few that didn't ignore him told him curtly they didn't know or care about the friends of Billy Patch. More than one had told him to go to hell.

With no leads on the three men, he had called at the surgery again. Again, he had received no response to his knocking.

One thing he did find out: cold-shouldered by strangers, yeah, but the saloonkeeper still took his money. It was not yet noon and he was sitting on the boardwalk with a fair quantity of liquor already inside him. But he was still in control of his faculties. Just.

His lit up his pipe and watched the smoke climb on the still air while he pondered on his next

course of action. Then his full bladder reminded
him he needed to use toilet facilities. OK, forced
by the call of nature to move he would take the
opportunity to get a few more drinks under his
belt. So much for all his good intentions.

As he stood up a buckboard came clattering
down the street. He could see a bloodied, young
man being tended in the back. From the shouting
going on as the wagon slewed round in front of the
doctor's surgery, the young farm worker had
sliced his hand with a scythe. Branston watched a
crowd gather and saw folks help down the injured
man. Goddamn! The surgery door opened and out
came the doctor. The bastard was in! Had just
been ignoring Branston's knocking was all. The
son-of-a-bitch.

His bladder was becoming real uncomfortable
but now he knew the doc was in, he didn't intend
breaking his surveillance so he decided to forgo
the niceties of the saloon urinal. He moved into
the neck of the nearest alley and relieved himself
against the planking of the saloon. Leaning at an
angle with his arm outstretched against the wall,
he kept his watch on the surgery front.

He buttoned his pants to the accompaniment of
loud tuts from an unexpected bevy of passing
womenfolk. As they swept by in their ground-
length dresses, he touched his hat in deference.
He smiled drunkenly, in the knowledge that the
gesture would have no effect in raising his
reputation which in this town was as low as the
females' hemlines. He crossed the thoroughfare
and heavy-footed through the now-unlocked door
of the surgery.

Three workmen were holding the young man on the table while the doctor tended to the hand. The wound was deep and Branston could see the operation was going to last some time so, unnoticed, he walked further into the building. A plush sitting-room, eating-room, kitchen. He moved into a study where he saw two empty whiskey bottles in the trash basket. The doc could have been having a party. But in the study?

He crossed to a bookcase. It was obvious the doc lived alone and didn't have a help as the shelves had an undisturbed veneer of dust. Except the middle shelf where the dust was mussed. He looked at the book titles. Nothing special. Novels, medical tomes. He took one out, then another. Lo, behind them: whiskey bottles! Full ones. Huh, he and the doc shared the same hobby!

Bourbon too. Top-dollar stuff. He took one, uncorked it and took a draught. Deep down he felt the new ingestion interacting with that already assimilated in the saloon.

He sat down at the desk and studied the room further while he imbibed. This man was a professional man and that was the trouble with a fondness for the juice. Branston was a bum and it didn't matter. All his drinking did was screw up his life. But drinking was bad in a doctor, a man who held life in his hands. The bottles being hidden demonstrated that the doc was aware of that.

Branston was aroused from his musings by the voiced agonies of the poor brush-popper being stitched up in the far room. He replaced the bottle and books and returned to the surgery. He leant

against the wall alongside a table supporting a
wash basin and pitcher, and lit up his pipe again.

Some minutes later the patient was being helped
out with a bloodied bandage round his hand. As the
crowd left the surgery the doc advanced towards
the wash basin. Branston tilted the pitcher and
filled the basin for him.

'Thanks,' the doctor said as he rinsed the redness
from his hands. Then, surprised that his visitor
had not made to depart with the others, he looked
at him with more interest as he dried his hands.
Then his face changed. 'Branston, ain't it? What do
you want?'

'Now that's funny, Doc. We've never met, yet you
know me.'

The medical man ignored the implication. 'Like I
said, what do you want?'

'I want to know more about how my brother died.
Sheriff, coroner. I can't get nothing out of nobody.
Tell me about it.'

'Some men brung him in. Like that young worker
you just saw. Only difference was, your brother
was dead. There was nothing I could do for him.'

'What was his condition exactly?'

'Neck was bust.'

'You sure of that?'

'I examined him on this very table.'

'Did he have any other injuries? Like mebbe he'd
fallen from some height rather than from a horse.'

'Nope. His condition was consistent with having
fallen from a horse. In this part of the world it is a
common occurrence, Mr Branston. Not every week,
but I've seen it many times.'

'These men that brung him in. Who were they?'

'Don't know. Reckon they were his buddies or workmates.'

Branston pondered. 'What time was this?'

'Late evening. Ten, eleven, something like that.'

'Did you check the body over, see if there were any other injuries?'

Doctor Adams started fidgeting with his tie. 'No need. Besides, like I said, it was late.'

'You check him over in the cold light of day the next morning?'

'No, he was taken to the undertakers first thing, as I recall.'

'So you wouldn't know if there were other injuries?'

'Such as what?'

'Such as a bullet hole.'

The doctor shook his head. 'Your brother died of a broken neck. I know a broken neck when I see one.'

Branston looked into the doctor's eyes. It was like looking into a mirror. Blood-shot eyes, puffed skin charted with broken blood vessels. 'And I know a drunk when I see one, Doc. Takes one to know one. It's my figuring that at ten o'clock at night you wouldn't know your ass from your elbow, never mind a broken neck.'

'Get out. I won't have my integrity questioned in this manner.' Stern-faced, the doctor moved with a sudden firmness and opened the door on to the street. Branston looked through the doorway and back at the doctor. The look in the man's eye told him there was nothing for it but to leave.

Once more on the boardwalk, Branston realized he was getting nowhere fast. Billy could have had his neck broken forcibly. Or been pushed off a rock. Could have been done by the bastards who brought him in. The doc said he didn't know 'em. If his brother had been carrying lead, the doc wouldn't have known that either. The only way to check for gunshot wounds would be by disinterring the body and Branston couldn't see Sheriff Settle and the coroner allowing that.

After a few minutes' contemplation he took off across the street to call on Meadows. 'Morning, Mr Branston,' the lawyer said, effusing a charm that competed with the sunshine outside, as Branston appeared. 'Take a seat, please.'

Branston dropped into a chair opposite the grimy window.

'You want me to arrange a sale of the property I presume,' Meadows went on, hooking his thumbs into his red suspenders.

When Branston said 'No' the lawyer's charm dissipated. 'What then?'

'Just information, if you please.'

'Yes?'

'Who owns the property that borders on mine?'

'The southern bit on the townside is still in the public domain and likely to stay that way. Then there's a short stretch along the northern pasture that's owned by Jesse Lowndes. You know, where the creek runs down?'

'Yeah.'

'Then the rest buts on to the Drucker spread. At least three-quarters of your border line. His property virtually surrounds yours.'

Branston nodded as he visualized the map. 'So one way of putting it is to say that the Double B splits his spread in two. Hmm, seems like the Double B is in his way.'

'Well, he did approach your brother on several occasions to discuss the possible sale of the Double B.'

Branston thought on the information. 'What's this Drucker like?'

'I would say he's a reasonable man. Big in the town of course. If you wanted to sell, a course I've already advised, he'd be the one to see. Offer you the best price, I reckon.'

'I ain't in the market. I was just wondering whose way the Double B is in. How far would he go to get it?'

'I don't get your drift, Mr Branston.' He did but he wanted the man to spell it out.

'The only support for Billy having an accident is the doc's evidence,' Branston went on. 'It was late at night when two unidentified bozos brought his body in. Not only was it dark but, from what little I know of the doc, I don't think he was sober. That ain't good enough for me. Billy could have been shot.'

'Wild and unjustified speculation, Mr Branston.'

Branston ignored the comment. 'I'm looking for motives. This Drucker. Seems like he could want the Double B bad if it's splitting his spread. How far would he go to get it?'

Meadows shook his head. 'He's a reasonable man but I don't think he'd cotton to having any fingers pointed at him. In your own interests, I'd advise you not to go roping Mr Drucker into your suspicions.'

'Which way's his ranch-house?'

'Due east of the Double B. But, Mr Branston, don't go causing trouble for yourself. He's a powerful man and he's got some hard guys working for him.'

'Doc Adams is dead.'

His hand on the door handle, Sheriff Settle was returning to his office with his deputy. 'Dead?' he asked, letting go and turning to the store-owner who had made the statement. 'Where?'

'In his study. He'd told me to collect some medicine. He wasn't in his surgery so I knocked on his study door. I found him slumped over his desk. He's dead all right. No heart beat. I checked.'

Minutes later the sheriff was making his own appraisal. There were no signs of violence. Just the dead man and an overturned glass with its spilled contents evaporated, making the place smell like a saloon.

'Lenny,' Settle said when he'd checked the corpse, 'ride out and get the doc from Pecos. We're gonna need medical opinion on this.' He turned to the store-owner. 'Gimme a hand to get the body over to the coroner's.'

Branston stepped out of Meadows' office and came face to face with Sheriff Settle. 'I've been making enquiries, Branston,' the lawman said sternly. 'Seems you visited the doc this morning.'

'Sure. Ain't no law against it, is there?' Branston threw back. 'Mind in this burg it might be. Nothing would surprise me round here no more.'

'What was your business with him?'

'What is this? You know exactly why I went to

see the doc. It was you who recommended me to see him. Wanted to find out more about Billy's death.'

'You say or do anything to upset the old man?'

'Told him I didn't think he did his job properly in certifying the cause of Billy's death. He didn't do no proper examination.'

'Well, looks like you've done it now with your damn questioning. The poor old doc's dead. Seems like a heart attack.'

Branston crossed the boardwalk and looked down, gripping the rail with both hands until the whites of the knuckles showed. 'Jeez, I was only talking to him, mebbe half an hour back.'

'Precisely. Looks like you were the last to see him alive. What state was he in when you left him?'

Branston had no reason to lie. 'I ain't gonna deny he was agitated. Said I was questioning his professionalism and told me to git the hell out.'

'That could be the cause. The way you shoot off your mouth, wouldn't surprise me.' He looked hard at Branston. 'Still, I can't arrest you for that. Just hope you got a conscience, that's all. And remember, I'm gonna be watching you.'

As the sheriff moved away, Branston remained with his hands gripping the rails and staring down at the planking of the boardwalk. The mess was getting messier. He looked up and down the street with a bruised look on his face. Huh, the townsfolk sure had another reason to be on the prod for him. Jeez, what next? One thing, he sure needed fortifying. He pushed hard away from the rail and went back to the saloon. What the hell.

He didn't know how many drinks later it was when a voice said, 'You don't have to tank yourself up with that stuff.'

He looked up. He could just about focus his eyes and make out Jenny. 'What the hell do you know?'

She sat down opposite him. 'I've heard about Doctor Adams. I know you feel guilty.'

'Horseshit.' The woman had been speaking in low tones but his coarse reply was heard by the audience around the saloon and they laughed.

'Don't you see?' she went on. 'That's the way they will want you to feel. You don't have to blame yourself for anything. Come on, Joe, the saloon is not the place for you.'

'What's all this guilt and blame stuff?' he mumbled.

She saw he wasn't to be moved immediately. 'Or maybe it is sorrow you are trying to drown. Are you feeling sorry for Billy Patch?'

He said nothing.

'Or yourself?' she persisted.

'I don't hold with all this analysing, missy. I drink 'cos I want to. Ain't no call for reasons other than that. Now you get your fantail outa here.'

'You don't deserve help.'

'An' I don't want none neither. Now git, young lady.' He tried to look authoritative but instead he keeled over and his head slumped on the table.

Jenny turned and surveyed the audience. 'Will someone help me out with him?'

'We'll help him outa town,' one man said. 'But apart from that, you're on your own Miss Jenny. Your old pa must be turning in his grave, you associating with the likes of him, his brother gun-running an' all. Now he's plumb talked the doc to death!'

NINE

'I'm banging my head against a wall here,' Branston said.

How Jenny had managed singlehandedly to manoeuvre a man of his size all the way to her house she didn't know, but she had. He'd slumped on the sofa and gone immediately to sleep. He'd stayed that way till late afternoon, coming to with a head like it had been jumped on by a couple of steers. She plied him with black coffee till it was coming out of his ears. Eventually the dead-head state was turning into the equally-familiar washed-out feeling of a hangover.

'Yeah, against a brick wall,' he went on as he sat at the table and stared into his umpteenth cup of coffee. 'A wall of silence.' He was angry: angry with the townsfolk for their lack of co-operation; and just as angry with himself for reacting to the problem by hitting the booze. He sat hunched in the chair, the fingers of one hand clenched around the bowl of his pipe while the fingers of the other drummed on the table. He looked up at Jenny across the table. 'There must be a crack of light someplace.'

'I've told you what little I know.'

'I don't hold anything against you, Jen. Let's face it, you're the only person in town who doesn't treat me like I got the plague.' He puffed on his pipe and reflected on the rising smoke in an attempt to calm himself. 'Anyways, how come you were about today? I thought only kids played hookey, not teachers.'

She smiled. 'Pull yourself together, Joe. It's Saturday. Even teachers are allowed some days off!'

He shook his head. 'I don't know what month it is, Jen, never mind the day of the week.'

'Drink isn't the answer to anything,' she said. 'We both know that.'

'Yeah, you're right.' He threw the remains of the coffee against the back of his throat. 'You know, there must be a lead from those who were close to Billy. There are three guys who were close to him. This Clem and Luke, they're unknown quantities. From what I can gather they came and went all the time. But Harleyson, the young kid who worked alongside him at the Double B, he's another matter. Why did he vamoose when he did? Now that's a question. You know, there might be a connection there.' Then, his eyes widened. 'In fact, he could be the one that killed Billy!'

Jenny was finding it hard to come to terms with this man. 'Joe, you're getting fanciful. Clutching at straws.'

'No. It would explain why he lit out so fast at such a time.'

'Oh, no, Joe. They got on well together. You didn't see them. I never heard a cross word between them.'

'That's as maybe. But Harleyson could have been paid to kill Billy. Have you ever thought of that? They say most murders are kin and friends.'

She tried to reject Joe's idea as gently as she could. 'I don't think that's plausible.'

'I gotta look at all possibilities, Jen. Maybe he headed for home. Do you know where he hailed from?'

'He made no secret of it. Buckler's Creek. Some thirty, forty miles east of here.'

'He got folks there?'

'Don't know about any pa but he talked of his ma still living there.'

Branston mused on the idea. 'Yes, I think I'll pay Buckler's Creek a visit. Sure as hell be more useful than sitting around town getting boozed.' He looked at the clock as he knocked out the dottle from his bowl. 'I'll take my leave now, Jenny. I've gotta pull myself together. With a ride ahead of me tomorrow, I need to get myself a good night's shuteye.'

He thanked her for rescuing him from the saloon and headed back to the Double B.

The dew was still thick on the meadow grass when Branston rode east out of the Double B the next morning. It was a long journey and the chestnut had gone low-headed by mid-afternoon when he came in sight of Buckler's Creek.

From a long way out, he could see the place wasn't much. But there was some life. High on a hill he could see farm hands working hay near a barn. He passed a buckboard laden with milk churns. In town he watered his horse and hitched it in shade.

There was no problem in locating Mrs Harleyson. She was well known and his first question of a
passerby elicited her whereabouts. She was one of
the town's washerwomen. He returned to his
horse, unhitched it and began walking it in the
direction indicated. He found the lady working a
pump outside a shack on the outskirts of town. She
had tousled grey hair swept largely unsuccessfully
to the back of her head, and the roly-poly matronly
figure that went with her age.

He tied his horse to a tree and advanced towards
her as she bent to pick up the filled buckets.

'Allow me, ma'am,' he said wresting the pail-
handles from her grasp. She looked up and wiped
the sweat along with strands of hair from her brow
with a podgy-fingered work-worn hand. She
appraised him for a second, shrugged and waddled
towards the shack like a mother-hen with her
chick behind her. The interior was hot and
clammy, pervaded with the smell of soap that
triggered memories for him of family wash-days as
a boy.

Inside, he knew why the old girl was sweating. It
was not only the labour. There were several large
vats of boiling water mounted on brickwork over
fires. She nodded to one and he emptied the
buckets into it.

'What is it, son?' she asked as he placed the
emptied pails on the floor.

'It is Mrs Harleyson, isn't it?'.

She used a large wooden stick to push down
recalcitrant clothes bent on resurfacing. 'Sure
thing. Stranger in town, ain't yuh?'

'Yes, ma'am.'

'You got washing you want doing?'

'No, ma'am. Name's Joe Branston. Brother of Billy Branston. I'm told your son worked for him.'

She laid down her stick. 'Yes, that's right. Billy Patch. Over in Brightwater. Got a horse ranch.'

'I was wondering where Dave is now?'

There was puzzlement on her face as she took a towel and wiped the moisture from her face and arms. She nodded to the door. 'Let's talk outside.'

Back in the cool air, Branston took off his stetson and wiped his own brow. 'Has he come back home?' he went on.

She looked even more puzzled. 'Ain't see'd hide nor hair of him for some time now. Got me worrying, 'cos he visited with me regular. You come direct from Billy Patch's place?'

'Yes, ma'am.'

'And he ain't working there now?'

'No, ma'am.'

'Should be. I thought he had a good steady job with Billy. Has your brother canned him?'

'No, it's a mite more complicated than that.' The wet heat was getting to Branston. 'Is there somewhere we can sit, ma'am?'

'There's a couple of chairs in the wash-house, son. Bring them out.'

A minute later they were seated outside on wicker chairs. 'You see, Mrs Harleyson, the fact of the matter is my brother's dead.'

'Mercy me,' the old woman exclaimed, throwing up her hands. 'I only met him the once but he was a charming fellow.'

'You haven't heard nothing about his passing?'

'No. Not in a month of Sundays. How's it happen?'

'Well, that's the point, Mrs Harleyson. No one really knows exactly how it happened.' Branston decided not to voice his exact suspicions to her. 'Thrown from a horse by all accounts. Davey's not about the place and I was wondering if he was all right. Wondered maybe something had happened to him as well.'

'This is sad news, indeed. I'm real sorry, Mr Branston.' She pondered for a spell. 'I brought my boy up honourable, Mr Branston. If there was trouble, an accident like you say, I'm sure Davey just wouldn't skedaddle.' She thought some more. 'He's a good boy. Was a rock to me when my husband died. Looked after the place. Mended what was needing mending. As he grew older I told him to stop thinking about me, get out and meet people. The world is a bigger place than Buckler's Creek and he should find out about it. Of course, it was hard to begin with. His father, God bless him, didn't leave much more than a red cent when he passed on, so I started washing.'

She nodded to the steam-vomiting doorway. 'It was Davey that outfitted the wash-house for me. Used to help me he did. But I told him: washing, laundering, ironing was no job for a man. After a spell, it was bringing in enough money for me to get by. Enough to pay for an old woman's groceries. Davey didn't need to stay here on my account.'

She looked townward. 'Then one day, your brother was riding through. They talked and Billy Patch offered him a job on his horse ranch. Davey didn't know much about wrangling and such but Billy said that didn't matter. The lad would pick it up.' She mused on the recollection for a few seconds. 'About a year ago, that was. Of course, I missed him. Ain't never lived on my own before. But Davey would come over every couple of weeks.'

She chuckled. 'Give me a few dollars, he would. I didn't want it 'cos I know a hand don't earn much. Board and pocket-money. But I took it for his self-respect. I still keep all the money he's given me in a jar. He can have that sometime, when he's needful of it.' She put her hand to her mouth, realizing she was being too open with a stranger. 'You won't tell him, will you? Nor nobody else.'

'Of course not, ma'am.' He stood up and took a long look around the place. There would be no answers for him here.

'I'm obliged, ma'am.'

She took his outstretched hand. 'If you see Davey, tell him his ma's waiting on him.'

He mounted up, touched his hat and gigged the chestnut. The woman seemed genuine enough. But one thing he'd learned in his not too long life: when it comes to folk, anything can happen. Appearances can be deceptive. Anybody can tell a tale. Was the old woman like that? One thing was for sure: if she was telling the truth he'd ridden into another blind gully. What leads had he got? Jenny knew sweet zilch. Everybody in town was clammed up tigher'n a drummer's ass. Billy's two pals had made themselves scarce. Now it looked like Davey had lammed it. There were no leads. Hell.

He looked skyward, then at his mount. The sun was low and his horse was stove-up. Was no chance of getting back to the Double B tonight. He tended to his horse's needs then found a drovers' shack where they were happy to take cents for a pallet. After a morose evening in the saloon he crawled into his bunk and subsided in depression.

TEN

Branston let the chestnut make its own pace back. He wasn't quite sure what he would be doing next. Seems like his questioning was just taking him round in circles. Maybe Billy had fallen from his horse and that was it. No mystery at all. Could be everybody was right, the sheriff, the doctor, the coroner, Jenny; and he was wrong. Could be the doctor's being affronted at the questioning of his competence was innocent, and the timing of his heart attack, a coincidence. Joe Branston was a plain and simple man, not used to having to wrench his brain this way and that over conundrums.

It was near noon and he was cutting down from the high country a few miles shy of the northern pasture when rifle fire racketed from the rocks and bullets whupped into the trunk of a tree that he was passing. The chestnut leapt forward catching him unawares and he toppled from the saddle. Winded, he got to his feet and staggered a spell, body instinctively cowed. Regaining his composure he looked for the source, squinting against the sun. But from his position his vision was limited. Then the assault stopped so he made

to chase his mount but the ruckus started all over
and bullets broke the ground ahead of him. He
took to cover, drawing his Colt. It went quiet
again. He couldn't see the bushwhackers nor what
they were doing. Could be reloading, or worming
their way to a better position.

Again the lull was short-lived. Bullets viciously
probed the greenery as the rifles searched him
out. Jeez, he was sure-as-hell pinned down. He
scanned the rocks. Up there somewhere. How
many bastards were there? God alone knew how
he could get out of this spot.

Suddenly behind him another rifle began a new
symphony of percussion. He didn't know who else
had joined the exchange and, at the moment, he
didn't care. He was simply gratified to see bullets
spanging from the rock edifice opposite him and
saw his chance. He loped down the open trail and
had made new cover before lead began to follow
him. Slowly he made his way up the rocks on the
near side.

Then, way above him, he saw a rife poking out
from a ledge. As he neared, the comforting smell
of cordite wafted down to his nostrils. He worked
his way higher till eventually he could make out a
figure prone on a ledge. Ejected shells bounced on
the rocky surface beside the young man as he
maintained his fusillade. Branston was surprised
not only by the intercession of a rescuer, but by
his age and colour. He was a young negro.

'Don't know who you are, mister,' the youngster
said, flashing a smile as he took another bead and
let fly, 'but seems to me two against one ain't
right.'

Branston took up position alongside him. Across the gap he could see figures edging their way back. There was no more firing from that side of the void. The young negro discharged a couple more bullets by way of finale, then turned to Branston. 'Reckon they're lighting out.'

Branston watched until the distant men had disappeared all together. 'Much obliged, mister.'

'Any idea who they were?'

'Nope, but they sure had the jump on me.'

'Figure they're just casual bushwhackers out for a few dollars. It ain't exactly law-abiding country out here.'

'In that case they'd a-sure been disappointed.'

The young man stuck out his hand. 'Hogan.'

'Joe Branston.' They shook hands. 'You got a first name?'

The negro's startling white teeth showed in a smile again. 'Guess I must have had sometime but it got kinda mislaid along the way. Folks allus called me Hogan as long as I can remember.'

'Well, Hogan. I was in luck that you chanced by. Otherwise don't know how that ruckus would have turned out. They'd got the drop on me.'

Hogan peered over the ledge. 'Your luck's still in, cowboy,' he said. 'There's your hoss. Ain't scooted far. Chewing the cud a couple of hundred yards down the trail.'

Branston looked down the ravine and confirmed the statement with satisfaction. 'Which way you headed?'

'South.'

'My place is a few miles south. Ain't much but I got some coffee and some cans of beans you're welcome to share, if you've a mind.'

'Sounds mighty inviting, Mr Branston. I ain't eaten for a day.'

Branston reclaimed his chestnut and they hit the ranch less than an hour later.

'Horses, eh?' Hogan said as they drew up near the corrals. He cast his eyes over the stock after he'd dismounted. 'Got yourself some good horse-flesh here, Mr Branston. I can see that.'

'You know horses?'

'Some.'

Branston looked at the sun. There was still a good section of the day left. 'Listen, I need to go into town for a spell. I wanna make a report to the law about the bushwhacking as soon as possible. You're welcome to use the facilities here while I'm gone.'

'That's mighty kind, Mr Branston. And mighty trusting to a stranger.'

'Reckon you mighta saved my life out there. If I can't trust a body that does that, who can I trust?'

In town he made for the sheriff's office and filled the lawman in on the attack upon him. 'I came straight here so that if you've a mind you could ride out and look the scene over,' he explained when he'd finished his recounting. 'Mebbe you can find some clues while there's still daylight.'

'No point,' the sheriff said. 'From what you've described of the locale of the incident it'd be like looking for a needle in a haystack.'

'You're not even gonna give it a whirl?'

'Did you get a look at them?'

'Nope. They had me cold-decked. It was all I could do to get under cover. It seems there were two of 'em. You got any ideas?'

'It could be anybody, Branston. Passing hard-cases, looking for easy pickings. Or someone could have followed you from Buckler's Creek. You tell me you went a-nosing out there. The way you handle that mouth of yours you could have upset somebody.'

'More likely somebody from these parts.'

'True. The Branston name ain't the most popular name around here, like I told you before.'

'I reckon there's another explanation. This Drucker who owns the land adjacent to mine. He wants the Double B. Taking pot-shots at me, that would be a way of trying to scare me off. The bushwhackers were using high-powered Winchesters so, before I took to cover, they could have ensured I was a goner. The fact they didn't means they were giving me a warning.'

'Well, take the warning. Sell up, like Meadows has advised yuh. Get outa town.'

'And that's what the law stands for?'

The sheriff remained unspeaking, unmoved. Branston thought he caught a look in the man's eye that said he had enjoyed being told someone was trying to weigh him down with lead.

'So long, Sheriff.'

The lawman's face was still unmoving granite.

ELEVEN

On the way back to the Double B Branston thought things over some more. His situation in Brightwater was sticky. Save for the girl everyone was against him so the odds on his getting to the truth of the matter were close to zilch. The way things were he was pretty sure he wouldn't be able to get a loan from the bank so, with little but jelly beans in his pocket, there was not much chance of him keeping the ranch going. He had been giving serious mind to the advice everybody had been throwing at him about getting out of town. But the sheriff's attitude riled him. There had to be some justice even if he had to make it himself. Was there a way of showing these bastards what he was made of?

He had plumb forgotten about Hogan and his mind was still on these matters when he got back to the ranch and saw the young negro sitting on the corral fence.

'What's the sheriff say?' the youngster asked as Branston swung from the saddle and tended to his horse.

'Couldn't be less interested. He didn't exactly laugh when I told him what had happened but I figure he found it amusing. For reasons I might get around to telling yuh, I ain't exactly welcome in Brightwater.' He unsaddled the chestnut. 'You eaten?' he asked as he dumped the rig on a saddle frame.

'Nope, thought I'd wait for you. Took some coffee is all.'

Branston walked over to the corral with the big stallion and leant on the fence. 'OK, Hogan, you tell me you know about horses.' He pointed to the big horse. It was the large-chested Arab. 'Break that one.'

'Is that all?' Hogan asked, raising his eyebrows. Branston wasn't sure the apprehension was real or mock.

Hogan shrugged his shoulders. 'You're the boss.' He went to his own rig and took out some small leather gloves from his saddle-bag. Then he made for the tack-room and came back with a couple of lengths of rope and a bridle. He dropped the bridle and a short rope to the ground, and coiled the longer length in his left hand, his right holding the noose at the slip knot. He scaled the fence and walked towards the horse, talking softly as he advanced. The stallion backed and began an agitated trot back and forth along the furthest fence.

'He's mean,' the young man said, halting well before the middle ground. 'I can see it in his eyes.'

'What do you expect me to test you with?' Branston said. 'A rocking horse?'

Then, as if he'd understood the conversation, the stallion charged the trespasser. It was a feint, for he swerved head down snorting as Hogan held his ground. It was the young man's turn to retreat. 'The next one's for real,' he said. 'I need a longer rope.' He was right. Before he had reached safety the horse charged and he just managed to clear the fence as the bronc reared, hooves chopping down menacingly.

Hogan was in the tack-room longer this time. Eventually he re-emerged with what he wanted and when he got to the corral he tested one of the gate stanchions. It was solid enough. 'This is gonna take some time,' he said. 'It'll be boring for an onlooker, if you've got things to do. Come back in half an hour if you like.'

'I'll stay,' Branston said. getting out his tobacco pouch.

'Suit yourself,' Hogan said as he vaulted the fence. Back in the corral he looped the rope round the post, then left it to approach the animal empty-handed. There then followed a game of cat-and-mouse, with Hogan closing in then diving for the fence as soon as the animal responded.

Half an hour, Branston was knocking out the dottle from his pipe when the black man looked across at him. 'Figure the critter's tired now,' he said. 'Or complacent. See the way he's making his challenges in a half-hearted manner. We'll soon see.' He gathered the two sections of rope and set off again towards the animal, trailing the two lengths. It was tricky but darting in and out he managed to loop the animal's neck. As the horse tried to charge, Hogan yanked hard on the rope such that it whipped tight round the post. The first tug tightened the noose close to the animal's jaw. Startled, the horse allowed himself to be pulled a few yards towards the post and away from Hogan. The bronco-buster took advantage of the animal's surprise to work his way fast along the length that he held before the horse careered off. The young man fetched up against the gate with a crash.

He leapt to his feet and cleared the fence as the angry animal charged at him. He threw several more coils round the post and the horse was pulled up sharp half way across the corral. Rope and post held. Then, each time the animal circled and the rope slackened, Hogan worked the rope shorter and shorter till eventually the brute was held fast against the post, back legs lashing.

'Looks easy don't it?' he grinned, sweat pouring from him. He left it that way until the animal became less agitated. Then he started speaking to it in a soft voice. The animal still snorted and its eyes rolled. But eventually there was quiet and the animal was stilled.

Hogan used his bandanna to wipe the sweat from his face, then took out the makings. 'Looks cute, don't he?' he said as he lit up. 'But don't let that fool yuh. There's plenty of go left in him. The critter's just biding his time. He's intelligent. Intelligent enough to know he's cold-decked for the moment.'

When he'd finished his cigarette Hogan stamped on it then resumed his talking to the horse. After a spell he picked up the rope bridle and, still talking, slipped it in place. The animal seemed to accept it until Hogan tried to get the bit between its teeth. It was only a rope bit but the horse didn't cotton to the thing and the man nearly lost a finger. He chuckled and persevered until eventually that task was accomplished.

Then he picked up the short length of rope he had brought earlier from the tack-room. From the safety of the fence he threw one end through the slats so that it fell on the ground beneath the horse without touching its legs.

'Hold the end for me, will yuh?' he asked. Back in the corral and resuming his one-sided conversation with the horse, he picked up the other end and laid it gently over the horse's back. The creature side-stepped away from the fence but there was enough play in the rope for Branston to keep his grip without it being dislodged from the animal. Outside again, the wrangler manoeuvered the two ends together and succeeded in knotting them to form a band around the forequarters of the horse's belly.

'When I'm on,' he said to Branston, 'free the rope.' He studied the horse for a second and added with a chuckle, 'or should I say if I get on.' Slowly he mounted the slats of the fence alongside the animal, maintaining his soothing sounds. Gingerly he eased himself on to its back. The animal stomped a little, snickered and rolled its eyes. When there was a lull in its pulling at its tethering, Branston uncoiled the rope.

The lull only continued for a few more seconds before the animal shot away. It circled the corral in an agitated gait. Gripping the bridle reins and rope cinch Hogan looked reasonably secure but the animal began to buck. The wrangler managed to stay on for two circuits but he was slipping badly and leapt clear before the animal threw him. Scrabbling to his feet he tore across the arena and vaulted the fence. But this time the animal calmed and didn't follow.

'That's enough for today,' Hogan said. 'He's had a taste of a rope, a bridle and a man on his back. But it's important he gets more handling tomorrow, just in case he thinks he's bested a rider on his back.'

'Let's eat,' Branston said heading for the main building. 'You have my admiration,' he continued as they stepped up on to the veranda. 'It's plain you do know something about horses. To put you in the picture, I've only just taken the ranch over and I'm thinking of keeping it going. There's complications here which I'll tell you about over dinner. The upshot is I can't pay anything to start with, but there's a job if'n you want it.'

Hogan chuckled, looking back at the horse. 'I did better'n I expected. Wouldn' wanna do that again in a hurry. He's got the look of a hard-boiled critter but I could detect in the eyes he's got the potential for a good temperament. Otherwise I wouldn' have tried to ride him first time.' He massaged his strained muscles. 'What you saw me do, I normally like to spread over a couple of days. That's the proper way of breaking. A little advance every day, building their confidence gradually. But you wanted to see something.'

'You did swell, my friend,' Branston concluded, opening the door. 'You a mind to stay a spell?'

'Let's talk, Mr Branston.'

TWELVE

The bunk-house had a dusty unlived-in look but the oil lamps brightened up the place. The two men were relaxing after a meal of eggs and hash that Branston had scratched together. Branston looked his guest over. He had a ragged workman-like appearance. He trusted the man and after he'd lit up his pipe he told him the story of his coming to Brightwater. About his brother, about his suspicions.

'Seems like folk wanna chase me off,' he said. 'Probably this Drucker guy on the next spread. Anyways, whoever it is, you've seen they ain't afeared to use lead. But that's firmed me up in wanting to stay. I've a mind to carry on where my brother left off. I've never had a place of my own, not like this. But there's the makings of a livelihood.'

Hogan fingered a pack of papers from his breast pocket and made a smoke. 'I hope yuh don't think I'm speaking out of order, Mr Branston,' he said after he'd flared a match, 'but it's plain to me you don't have too much savvy about the horse business.'

'You hit the nail on the head.'

'Well, if you're aiming to make a go of this place there's decisions to be made. There's several ways of running a horse business. Looking around I figure your brother dabbled in all of them. You can go out and catch mustangs. For that you need a good tracker. Ain't always as easy as it might seem to detect that a herd has gone by. You need a good man to read sign: when and how big the herd was. It means long months in the saddle. Horses don't grow on trees; otherwise there'd be no business in it. You need a crew of wranglers to build fences across canyon mouths. Men you can trust. You need mustangers for herding. Then, you got a big herd of mustangs corralled you need a whole team of bronco-busters. That's one way.

'Another is to breed your own hosses. That way you don't need such a big crew. But you need a good spread with plenty of forage and, most important, you need time. You need breeding skills so you know what you're aiming for when you cross stock. It's just as easy to bring out the bad from both sides of a foal's parents as it is to bring out the good. Sure, breeding might make a man a fortune eventually, especially if he strikes lucky with a strain, but it ain't no way to make a quick buck.

'Then a man can just buy and sell hosses. Plain and simple horse-trading. The link man between those that have horses and those that need 'em. That needs cash up front and a good eye for the animals 'cos decisions need to be made fast. A guy doesn't wanna end up with dud hosses, mounts with illnesses it ain't plain to see, or critters with a hidden mean streak that ain't gonna be no use

to their owner. Word soon gets around if your
merchandise can't be trusted.'

Branston looked at his companion. 'You sure got
an old head for a young un. Where'd yuh learn all
this?'

'Was born on a plantation. Carolina.' He raised
his hands. 'You can see the colour of my skin. I
don't have to tell you what the conditions were.
My life was cotton, same as all my folk. Anyways,
I had this flare for horses. The master spotted it
early on, said I must have been born in the saddle.
Took me off the land, set me to looking after his
stables. Even had me racing thoroughbreds.
Anyways, I became his favourite and that didn't
set well with my friends, you know. Called me an
Uncle Tom. Come the war I was a wrangler with
the Confederacy. At the end of the war I took my
chance and left. Drifted west. One thing I've
found, there's allus a need out west for somebody
who can work horses.'

'How come you're still drifting?'

'Another thing I've found, some folks don't like a
black man who knows better'n they do. There's
allus some poke in the crew on the prod for a fella
like me.' He shrugged. 'But I get by.'

'If you stay on here a spell I can't pay you much.
In fact nothing at all to start with. I've told yuh
my story.'

Hogan chuckled again. 'I ain't bothered about
that. As long as I got some grub in my belly and
nobody ain't heaping manure on me, I'm satisfied.
If I ain't satisfied here I'll move on. Is that square
enough for you?'

'Like I said, you sure got an old head.'

Hogan yawned. 'Now, if you don't mind, Mr Branston, I gotta lay down this old head someplace afore it drops off.'

'Yeah, we're going to need some more men,' Hogan said the next day after they had ridden around the spread. 'Like I said last night. The place and your plans are small scale but two can't handle it. That's going to be a problem from what I understand of your situation. The way the town is all-fired up against you even if you could pay there wouldn't be any takers.'

'I been thinking on that,' Branston said. 'You got anything against working with Mexicans?'

Hogan laughed. 'Not if they ain't got nothing against me!' He raised his hands from his saddle horn and looked about in mock incredulity. 'But where the hell you gonna get Mexicans?'

Branston smiled. 'I can see you ain't too good on geography. Mexico, where else?' He spotted the puzzled look on the black man's face. 'I know what I'm doing,' he went on. 'I'll leave tomorrow but first I aim to ride out to Drucker's place. Tell him face to face the way I feel.'

'You think that's wise?'

'I'm a man who puts his cards on the table. 'Sides, if I'm gonna be around a spell, I gotta meet up with my neighbours sometime.'

'You want me to ride along?'

'No, thanks. I've taken you on for what you know about horses. This other business is mine.'

THIRTEEN

Later Branston rode out to the Drucker spread. He was looked at coldly by the hands but allowed to pass. It was plain they knew who he was. As he proceeded he gave them equal scrutiny, hoping that he might see someone familiar, a shape maybe that he had seen against rocks. But his attackers of the other day had been so far away and well hidden that he knew there would be little chance of that.

At the ranchhouse he was ushered into the study where Karl Drucker was seated at a desk. The man was aware of his visitor but he didn't look up from his task of sorting through papers. Some documents he laid on a pile, others he ripped in half and dropped into a bin at his side. It was clear he would not welcome any interruption that diverted him from his task.

Branston looked around the room. It was finished in polished wood adorned with expensive ornaments: miniature statues on tables and shelves, highly decorated china plates fixed to the walls.

'I've been expecting you, Branston,' Drucker said as he consigned a final document to the bin

with a flourish. The words were clearly enun-
ciated but heavily laden with an accent. He was
around fifty, solidly built with a Germanic
squareness to his features. He pushed the pile of
documents away from him and flicked a hand as
instruction for his men to leave. The ranch hands
hesitated for a moment but a second gesture
caused them to retire and close the door. Drucker
indicated a seat. 'Put your bones on a chair.'

Branston sat.

'Now tell me what you want of me,' the older
man said, settling back in his sumptuous swivel
chair. The words were delivered in a matter-of-
fact tone but Branston looked at the brown eyes
and saw they had an intensity that indicated the
speaker was a dangerous man to buck.

Despite his assessment of the no-nonsense
character of the man, Branston decided to be
blunt. 'My brother was killed. I reckon he was
murdered.'

'I heard scuttle-butt about your opinions. And
your activities. Let me hear from your own lips
how you see the situation.'

'Billy only had a small spread but it's plumb in
the middle of the valley cutting it in half. A damn
nuisance to anybody owning the land on either
side. Ownership rights in the territory ain't been
officially registered yet. It's still a free-for-all.
When a Land Office is set up in town and official
registration is instigated ownership will legally
lie with whoever has deeds to land or, failing that,
whoever is in occupation at the time of enforce-
ment. I figure whoever killed Billy did so to get his
piece.'

'So?'

'You own the land on either side of Billy's plot.'

Drucker adjusted his posture and straightened the expanse of good suiting that encompassed his frame. 'You trying to tell me something?'

'Figure it out for yourself.'

Drucker ruminated for a spell. Then, 'I don't cotton to your inference, Branston.'

'And I don't cotton to being shot at.'

'I heard about that. An unfortunate business but you came out unscathed.'

'Only because a fellow handy with a gun happened by and kept them at bay until I could get to cover. Could have been an attempt to get me out of the way permanent, same as Billy.'

Drucker grunted. 'Seems to me if someone aimed to get you out of the way by jumping you like that they would have made sure it was done properly. Mebbe somebody was warning you of something. From what I been hearing you been ruffling a few feathers.'

'Well it didn't even scare me off. In fact, it hardened my resolve. I may as well tell you I aim to keep the Double B going despite what you or anyone else does.'

Drucker grunted again. 'That's your privilege, fella. But I'm telling yuh, that shooting at yuh was none of my doing. I am a businessman but I also have principles. Sure your spread sits awkward for my affairs and I'd welcome a chance to buy it. Had discussions with your brother. You want to sell in his stead, we can talk about a price.'

Branston shook his head. 'Like I said, I'm setting down roots.'

Drucker nodded. 'OK, you don't want to sell. I can live with that. I know what it means to set down roots. I've done it myself. Came here, started my spread from scratch, years before your brother came.'

He rose and walked to the window. 'Land wasn't fenced. He rides into town and carved out his little bit. It was free range, nothing I could do. He's gone now, you're here. We can be neighbours as friendly as you want to be.'

He returned to his desk and looked hard at his visitor. 'Having said that, I tell you one more thing, Branston, and I'll only tell you once. Your brother's death was exactly how it looks, an accident. Furthermore I had no part in your bushwhacking yesterday. That is all. We have nothing left to say to each other.' On that he bellowed a name and a plug-ugly heavy-footed into the room. Drucker made a get-moving gesture. 'See that Mr Branston leaves the outfit safely.'

FOURTEEN

Back at the ranch Branston ferreted through Billy's business documents and found the telegraphic addresses of military purchasers in the state. He wrote out a list which he stuffed in his jacket pocket. Then he made an inventory of the stores. He discovered another cupboard with provisions in the kitchen. There was cornmeal, flour and a supply of jerky, enough to get by on.

'I aim to ride to Mexico tomorrow,' he told Hogan when he'd finished his assessment. 'Figure on rustling up those extra hands, I was telling you about. It'll take some days there and back. Can you manage till then?'

'No problem, boss,' the young man said.

'There's enough canned food around the place so you shouldn't starve.'

'I can get on with some work too,' the youngster said. 'There's four horses ready for breaking. I can start them while you're away.'

Branston set out early the next morning, trailing a remuda of two for speed. One thing he wasn't short of was horses. On his way through Brightwater he sent out cables to Rangers headquarters in Austin and various military posts announcing he was in business for horse trading. Once the last one had been tapped out he set out for the Rio Grande. With a bit of luck, there might be a firm order or two when he got back. If not, at least the authorities would know he was in business.

The weather was kind and he crossed the plateau without trouble. When he got to Hernan's he stayed over and helped harvest the green cows while Hernan continued the journey into the interior to fetch the other two vaqueros. Carlos and Miguel were just as happy as Hernan to see their old gringo friend. As Branston had expected they were still without employment and jumped at the chance of trying their luck with the Americano even though he couldn't guarantee wages for a spell. None had been north before but they knew livestock and he could trust them.

A week passed. He had returned to the Double B and the Mexicans were settling in. With four men about the place, the work was becoming manageable and Branston looked forward to making the business viable. But the drawback was still cash. He was worried about not being able to pay his men but their hearts were in the right place and there was no immediate problem. However the matter came to a head when Jesse Lowndes, the owner of the spread which bordered the northern pasture, paid a visit asking for payment for the water coming down the creek.

Lowndes related how he'd wanted to divert the water a couple of years ago but, knowing it would deprive the Double B, he had talked it over with Billy. They had come to a financial arrangement, the current payment of which was now due. Branston checked Billy's files and found a receipt for the previous year. Seemed like a legitimate claim, but he hadn't got the required fifty dollars. He remembered Meadows had warned him there would be bills coming up. Lowndes said he was understanding and would allow him a couple of weeks but he needed either the money or the water so, if the bargain wasn't honoured, he'd have to divert the water away from the creek for his own purposes.

Used to being given orders all his working life, this wheeler-dealing was new to Branston. But there was no escaping it: he would have to learn how to be a businessman. So he figured he'd have to try the banks, half-guessing what his reception would be. On the basis of nothing ventured, nothing gained, he rode into town and reined in outside the Cattleman's Bank.

His interview with the president was short and unfruitful. From there he went to the Mercantile Bank but was dismissed by a clerk. Stepping out of the town's third and last bank with the instruction never to set foot in the establishment again, he came face to face with the sheriff.

'Been aiming to see yuh, Branston,' he said. 'Where yuh been? Thought mebbe you'd cleared out.'

'No such luck, Sheriff. Been away on business. Pulling in labour.'

'Ha, the negro and Mexes I heard about,' the lawman said with a sneer. 'Waal, that ain't gonna set well with some folks round here. I'll tell yuh that.' He nodded towards the Law Office. 'Let's have a parley, Branston.' Inside the small room he threw his hat on to a stand and rubbed his hair with his hand. 'How you doing with the banks?'

'No dice as you well know.'

'Like I've told yuh, folks don't want you settling.' He dropped into his chair. 'Now, we ain't got much law hereabouts, Branston, but what we do have is me. Now, I know you're upset over your brother but that ain't no excuse for going round disturbing folks.'

'Suppose you're talking about Drucker? Reckon I break wind in these parts and everybody knows it.'

'Branston, I gave you the particulars on your brother's case. He was guilty and saved public money by having an accident. That's all there is to it. Going around, shooting off your mouth the way you've been doing, all that does is ruffle feathers. Ain't no percentage in that for you, me nor nobody else. If you don't get my drift, I'm telling you to lay off.'

Branston remained immobile. Then, 'Guilty? You keep telling me Billy was guilty of gun-running. But just 'cos you keeping saying something don't make it true. What makes you so sure-fire it's Billy?'

'We told you we found guns from the same shipment in the Double B ranchhouse.'

'And I told yuh they could have been planted. Evidence like that ain't legal until it's stood up against investigation in court.'

'We got a witness, too.'

'Again, whether what a witness says is acceptable in a case has to be shown in a court.'

'Well, that's denied us now. With your brother having the accident. I ain't never heard of no dead man being tried. You just gotta face things. And if you don't lay off like I'm asking, I'm gonna have to take some action.'

'This witness, what was he a witness to?'

'A wagon heading out for where there was nothing but desert and Comanches. Went in loaded, came out empty. There was three men with the wagon. The descriptions of two could fit in with your brother's buddies, Luke and Clem. But playing your game of devil's advocate, the descriptions ain't good and there's a chance they might not have stood up in court. They were wise enough not to show themselves in town very often, so nobody knows much about their appearance. But the third was more than a passing description of your brother in terms of physique and clothes. And he had a patch over the left eye.'

'Hog shit! You need more than that. Eye-patches ain't uncommon. 'Sides, anybody can put a patch over their eye. Just to confuse matters or throw suspicion on somebody. Who's the witness anyways?'

'You wouldn't know him. And I ain't giving you his name 'cos I ain't having you harass him. It fell that he crossed them on the trail.'

'And what exactly did he see?'

'When they'd passed he looked back. There was a tarp covering the load but it had slipped. Saw a rifle box. Seemed suspicious at the time 'cos there weren't no habitation out that way, it being wild country an' all. But, you know how folks are, didn't figure it was any of his business. That was afore the Indians started up. After the uprising, we were putting together the pieces and he came forward with his account.'

'Could he positively identify Billy?'

'The patch was the surest thing.'

Branston exhaled noisily. 'So you were all fixed up to put a noose round Billy's neck and all you had was the casual observation of some trail bum. Huh.'

He headed for the door. 'Well, if that's all, Sheriff?'

'Just watch your step and remember: stop being a burr under folks' saddles.'

The sun's last blushes tinted main street as Branston stepped outside. He leant on the rail and looked up and down the street while he pondered the situation. His dearest wish now was to stay: to clear up the mystery of Billy's death and to get Billy's ranch going again. But he was no businessman and he'd got four men working for him on nothing more than a promise. But he couldn't expect them to do that for ever without pay. And he'd gotta pay for water rights. Soon he would need to buy good oats for the horses. And Meadows had said something about local taxes. There was more to running a business than he'd first thought. Where the hell could he get finance to get the ranch going? He strode along the boards and pushed through the batwings of the saloon.

As he stood at the bar and ordered a beer he remembered his self-imposed temperance pledge. That had gone down the chute his first night in Brightwater. What the hell, he needed to wash the taste of that mealy-mouthed sheriff and his goddamn town out of his system. He took his jar to a seat and began his cleansing operation.

It was countless beers later that he noticed Meadows at the bar. He pulled himself to his feet and walked ungainly across the room. 'You're my lawyer,' he slurred. 'You're supposed to advise me. So, advise me where I can get the cash to run Billy's outfit.'

'I've already told you, Mr Branston, it is my considered opinion that you sell up and leave. I can handle the sale for you.'

'Huh, for peanuts.' Branston took another swig. 'A damn useless lawyer you make. You don't know nothing. The one person in town who should be able to help and you're as useful as tits on a bull.'

Meadows looked him over and was not pleased with what he saw. 'I don't care for your manner, Mr Branston.' He took his small glass of whiskey to a table and sat down.

Branston lumbered after him and dropped heavily in a chair opposite. 'And I don't care for you period.'

'I'm not staying here to listen to this,' Meadows said, rising.

Branston grabbed the man's lapel and yanked him down to the chair again. 'You'll go when I say so, you scheming buzzard. You only want me to go so you can get a cut. I reckon you're in with them. The sheriff, doc, Drucker.'

Meadows easily wrested the drunken man's hand from his coat and rose a second time. Branston's hand flailed in thin air. 'Damn shyster,' he muttered but before he could summon up his resources the lawyer had gone. Branston glanced around and his eyes met the disapproving looks of the rest of the room's occupants. He threw the vestiges of his drink against the back of his throat and stood up. 'Damn town,' he grunted and staggered to the door.

Outside he fell from the boardwalk and sprawled in the dust in the darkness. Unseen hands grabbed him. 'Get the drunken bum offa the street,' someone said, 'afore he causes somebody to pitch from their hoss.' He felt himself being hauled on to the walkway where he sat slumped. He stayed that way until he could muster enough strength to sort out his horse and clamber into the saddle.

He sure hoped the critter knew the way back.

FIFTEEN

There are ways and ways of being woken up. One is by distant birdsong. Another is by the gentle stirrings of a woman's body. One way Branston didn't cotton to was being pitched into the conscious world by the breaking down of a door. But that morning he had no choice in the matter.

He rolled out of bed but his lack of co-ordination caused him to stumble and he lay on the boards, squinting at the sunlight which flooded through the gaping hole where the door had been.

He could make out Sheriff Settle and his deputy.

And the four hand-pistols levelled at him.

'Get your pants on, Branston. You're taking a ride into town.'

Branston got up from the floor and cradled his head in his hands. The room stank of the overnight effects of sour beer on his body and the old hammer was using his skull as an anvil again. He was on a familiar trail where every day is another slice of hell.

'What fer?' he asked when he had composed himself enough to form words.

'Fer killing Meadows.'

Branston grunted cynically. 'Meadows? Dead?'

'Being dead usually goes along with being killed,' the sheriff said nudging at Branston's chest with his pistol. 'Move.'

'Meadows?' Branston persisted. 'How?'

'Gunshot.'

Branston pulled on his pants. 'And you aim to pin it on me?'

'Where's your gun?'

Branston scanned the room then pointed to his gunbelt which he had dropped carelessly to the floor in his collapsing towards the bed some time late last night. Or it might have been early this morning. The holster was empty. He forced his mind to focus on the matter and then he vaguely remembered unknown hands hauling him off the street when he'd staggered out of the saloon. The state he had been in, the last thing he would have noticed was someone relieving him of his iron. He'd only made it to the ranch through the good sense of his horse.

'What's going on, boss?' It was Hogan appearing at the door hitching his belt. The Mexicans were behind him rubbing the sleep from their eyes.

'Stay outa this,' the sheriff said. 'Law business.'

'Listen, Sheriff,' Branston grunted. 'Ain't no way I could have shot anybody last night. I could hardly stand, never mind aim a gun. You ask the boys here.'

'That's right, Sheriff,' Hogan said. 'He was real drunk. He wouldn't have been capable of doing what you say.'

'*Si, señor*,' Hernan said. 'He wouldn't have made into bed without our aid.' He slapped his forehead.

'You never did see someone so drunk, *señor*.'

'You bozos work for him,' the sheriff said. 'Your word don't count.'

'OK,' Branston said, trying to pull his thoughts together. 'Ask the folk in the saloon.'

'We did. The one thing they do know is that you had an argument with the deceased. They'll all swear to that; and to you putting your hands on the poor fella.'

Branston stood up. 'I suppose my gun was found at the scene?'

'Yeah,' the sheriff confirmed, 'making it an open and shut case.' He turned to his deputy. 'See to his horse getting saddled up, Lenny.'

Outside, Hogan held his horse while he mounted. 'They will not be able to make this charge stick, Joe. Meantime, don't worry about the ranch. We can handle things here.'

The sheriff laughed as he watched Branston settle ungainly into the saddle. 'You, a businessman? The only thing you can handle is looking into the bottom of a tankard.'

From then on no words were exchanged giving ample time for Branston to think as they rode into town. The sheriff was right. He was no businessman – but he knew enough to know that every city and town had a businessman's clique. An elite that met behind closed doors and fixed politics and the working climate for everybody else. That group, consisting of bankers, politicians, local government officials, tradesmen, was the seat of power in a town. A guy with a business who wasn't in that group and tried to play it straight would have to have more than his fair share of luck to survive. Even more so if the caucus was positively against him. And this lot was against him, against the Branston name. The more he thought about it, the more his mind circled the possibility that such a group would have no difficulty in eliminating somebody they wanted out of the way. They could have fixed Billy's murder. That would explain a lot of things. Like the brick wall he kept running into.

Had the doctor died as a result of being faced with his complicity? And what about Meadows? Was he a member of the clique but had had a twinge of conscience? And they'd got rid of him, framing Branston for it.

Neat. Killed two birds with one stone.

SIXTEEN

The room was half in shadow, the only light the kerosene lamp on the desk. The sheriff was at the window, holding back the curtain looking at the rain. It had been three hours since he'd dismissed his deputy to take the night-shift himself.

'Damn rain,' he muttered through the cigar clamped between his teeth. Dispersed put-put sounds behind him pinpointed where the roof was leaking. He'd requested the town committee to fix the thing but they were dragging their feet. There was a time when he could have repaired it himself but nowadays his joints creaked too much for him to go clambering over roofs. He'd sent his deputy up to see what he could do but all the greenhorn had succeeded in doing was dislodging more shingles so that there were even more leaks now. Damn half-ass wasn't all that hot at being a deputy either.

He returned to his desk and looked disinterestedly at the laid-out deck of cards. He sat down, brushed away a length of cigar ash that dropped down his shirt-front and resumed his game of patience.

In the back cell Branston lay on the bunk which

he had had to move to escape the rain splattering in through the open window. The bars stopped him getting out of the place all right but not the rain and wind from coming in. He'd had no luck in trying to sleep, his initial indignation at being hauled away in the early hours of the morning compounded by minor irritations which had grown in the darkness. The damp bedding on the bunk for a start. And then the warm aroma of the sheriff's cigar filling the building, reminded him that he hadn't picked up his beloved pipe when he'd been arrested that morning.

There was a knock at the door. The sheriff looked up quizzically and stubbed out his cigar. 'Who's that?' he shouted

'Lenny.'

The sheriff rose, looking at the clock on the wall as he crossed the room. What could his deputy want at one o'clock in the morning? He turned the key in the door but was pushed back as the door burst open. He staggered and before he could react there were two masked men in the room, six-shooters levelled.

'Keep your hand from your gun, Sheriff,' one warned as the other closed and relocked the door.

The sheriff looked the men over as his hands rose. He didn't recognize the critters. They weren't local but somehow they knew enough to use the name of his deputy.

Branston was standing equally inquisitive at the bars of his cell. What the hell was going on?

'Keep them hands high,' the first masked man continued while the second advanced and wrenched the sheriff's pistol from its holster. The cartridges were shaken from the chamber. 'Now give my pardner the keys.'

The second man threw the emptied gun aside on the desk and took the keys. He fingered through them as he moved back to the cell. 'Your lucky night, pardner,' he said, selecting the largest key. It fitted and a second later the iron door clanked open. 'You got belongings to collect?' he asked as put his head round the open door of the tack room opposite the cell. He extricated a length of rope from a dusty pile of oddments.

'Nope,' Branston said as they walked towards the front office. 'They yanked me outa bed. Ain't even got my hat.'

The man chuckled. 'Ain't ever known the law to be considerate. And we couldn't even get you a hoss. Yours will be in the livery but it'll be too risky trying to get it. Might wake the ostler. So, you're gonna have to move your ass. Once you're outside this building you're on your own, pal. They're gonna be after you with all they got come daylight.'

Out front he took the sheriff's hat and jacket from the wall and slung them at Branston. As he did so Branston caught sight of a star tattooed on the back of his hand. It was vaguely familiar but Branston couldn't place it. 'It's sheeting down outside,' the fellow went on. 'That'll give you some cover. Ain't gonna be too many nosy bastards out in this weather this time of morning. You got about four hours of darkness left. You should have a good start.'

He took a length of rope from a hook on the wall and indicated for the lawman to sit in the chair.

Still at an utter loss, Branston donned the jacket and hat. 'Why are you doing this?'

'What's the matter?' the first man said as his comrade coiled the rope around the seated peace officer. 'You're grateful, ain't yuh?'

'Dunno. Could be I might be heading for bigger trouble out there. Just like to know what this all about.'

'Listen,' the man with the tattoo said. 'Let's say mistakes have been made. You've been framed good. There's no way you'd beat this rap.'

The sheriff was soon trussed up in his chair, his mouth gagged with his own bandanna. The first man holstered his gun. 'Don't stick around,' he said to Branston as he unlocked the front door. 'Get outa the territory, back where you came from. Mexico, wasn't it?' Slowly he opened the door and looked furtively out. 'Clear, pal.'

Branston stepped outside followed by his two rescuers and stood in the dark of the porch. 'You gonna tell me who I have to thank?' he said as he looked up and down the street.

'No need,' the first man said. 'Now, git. Don't spit on good fortune.'

Branston turned up the collar of the jacket. 'Well, whatever the reason and whoever you are, thanks.'

'Best of luck, pal,' the second said as the two disappeared into the water-curtained darkness.

As he watched them go he had a thought that caused him to hesitate. Maybe this whole thing was part of the power group's plan. That he gets shot while trying to escape. Hell, there wasn't much he could do about it now he was out. Just have to take his chances.

He pulled the hat brim down against the rain and headed off along the street which would take him to the Double B, the same direction as the masked men. It was hard going as the thoroughfare had turned to mud. His mind raced. Where should he go? It would take him some time to get to the ranch on foot. Once there he could pull some provisions together and light out with a couple of horses. Doubtless the Double B would be the first place the sheriff would look once he'd got his posse together but by then he would be miles away.

He glanced left and right as he ran. Here and there a window was lit but thankfully there was nobody on the street.

He passed an alley and he saw three sorry-looking horses standing in the rain. His two rescuers were untying them and preparing to mount. He paused for a second. Why three horses? They'd said they hadn't got a spare for him.

He'd just resumed his progress down the street when, suddenly, he was startled by a flame of light in a doorway on the opposite side. A match flared briefly outlining a man's face as he lit a cigarette. But the fugitive was looking through too much sleeting rain for anything more than the most fleeting of images to register and a split second later the doorway was dark again.

For a second Branston panicked. The man had lit his cigarette one-handed. There had been a gun in the other. Was he being set up to be shot as an escaped fugitive? The man had obviously seen him but didn't move. From his vantage point in

the doorway the watcher must have seen the
three men leave the sheriff's office. Even in the
rain he must have seen that two of them were
masked. And seen the waiting horses. A bystan-
der who didn't want to get involved? The world
was full of them. If he was, Branston for once was
grateful.

But with a gun in his hand? Either way
Branston wasn't gonna hang around to find out
and he stepped up his momentum down the
street. He glanced back once and saw a huddled
shape crossing from the doorway to the alley. The
man for the third horse?

SEVENTEEN

It was an advantage he had become familiar with
the locality otherwise he would never have found
his way in the rain and darkness. He was soon out
of town and heading cross country along the trail.
Having to trudge through mud kept the pace slow
but he consoled himself with the thought that at
least the rain would cover his trail, before he
reminded himself once again that the ranch would
be the first place the sheriff would look anyway.

All the more reason for him to keep moving,
denying himself even a few minutes' rest-up
under a tree. His mind ran to the ranch ahead. He
knew he could trust the Mexicans but what about
Hogan? He'd have to trust him too. There was
every chance that getting his horse and provisions
ready would would wake the men. He pondered on
whether they would get into trouble when the law
turned up. Would the badge-carriers see them as
his accomplices? His crew could be in trouble if
the sheriff or anyone in his posse had a thing
against Mexicans or negroes. They were in the
kind of country where that was a distinct
possibility. Hogan would have to make his own
decisions. The *vaqueros* would have to head back

to the Terra Fria.

And what about himself? OK, he gets horses
and provisions, then where? Mexico again? Jeez,
he didn't know; he'd think that through later. As
he wiped the rain from his eyes he pondered on
the mess his life had been, and still was. He
pondered further on the Double B. The place had
looked innocuous enough on that first day when
he had ridden up; but it sure had jinx
associations. First there was Billy turning bad,
and now him on the lam.

He staggered round a bend, his breathing
coming hard. Still a couple of miles to go and he
was tiring. There was no let up in the rain and, in
the morning's early hours, it had a cold edge to it.
Nothing for it: he'd have to rest.

Suddenly his foot hit a rock, something solid in
the quagmire that was supposed to be a trail, and
he keeled over. His shoulder slammed into the
ground, he rolled over and for a second he lay on
his back, the rain smashing into his face.

He cursed. Couldn't lie like this, had to keep
moving. He made to get to his feet but winced in
the process and slumped again into the mud. Jeez,
his ankle was painful. He tried to rub it but the
action was ineffective through the leather of his
boot while at the same time pain came from his
jarred shoulder. After another unsuccessful
attempt at walking he hopped to the side of the
trail and slumped his behind on to a hillock.
Cow-punching on the range meant that falls from
his horse were not a new thing to him, but it had
been a long time since he'd incapacitated himself
like this. And at what a time.

Hell, what next? He'd lost track of time and distance but he knew he hadn't travelled far from town. Maybe a mile at the most. He grunted as he tried his leg again. There was no way he could make the ranch in this condition. How long would it take the sheriff to get free? Maybe he was rounding up a posse at this very minute. Where else could he go?

Then he thought of Jenny. She was the only one in town who'd shown him any understanding. And her place was the only one he stood a chance of getting to before daybreak. Cursing again, he rose, and limped back along the trail.

How long it took him to get to her house he didn't know. The rain had let up slightly, but not much. He tried the front and back doors but they were locked. He threw a couple of pebbles at an upstairs window, but he didn't know which was her room. Then he found a downstairs window slightly open. He gripped the underside and managed to ease it up high enough to provide a reasonable space. He pulled himself up and squirmed through the gap, wincing as his bad leg took some weight. Inside he closed the window and took off his hat, wiping his brow and hair.

He moved cautiously through the darkness, hands in front of him. He caught the shin of his lame leg against a chair which fell over with a clatter. Seconds later Jenny's voice came from upstairs. 'Who's there?'

He took a careful step in the direction of her voice. 'It's me. Joe.' He felt the newel at the bottom of the stairs and it gave him his bearings. There came the scratching of a match, followed by a faint glow at the top of the stairs.

'Joe?' Then she was there, peering down. He stayed slumped against the newel as she made her way down. He caught the scent of her perfume as she neared.

In the glow of the kerosene her eyes were puffed from sleep. 'What's happened?'

'Got sprung from jail.'

'Jail? What were you doing in jail?'

'Meadows, the lawyer. He was killed tonight. Someone's trying to frame me. My gun was used. Sheriff won't take my word for anything.'

'How did you get out?'

'That's another odd thing. Two strangers with masks bust in. In fact, I figure there was three in total as there was another standing in a doorway. He acted as though he was with them. Queer set-up all round.'

He eased himself down on to a step. 'Couldn't get my horse. Had to walk it. Believe me, Jenny, I didn't intend to involve you, but I've crooked my leg. Couldn't make it out of town. You've got every right to kick me out.'

'Don't be silly. Come into the parlour. Let's have a look at it.' She helped him stand and felt the wetness. 'My, you're soaked. You'll have to get those clothes off.'

The fire was low in the hearth and she built it up while he lowered himself into a chair and took the weight off his leg. It was a hard wooden chair but it felt good. He eased off the jacket as the flames began to bite the new kindling with a cheering crackle.

It was half an hour later. His clothes were

draped over a wooden clothes horse before the fire and he was wrapped in a blanket sipping a second cup of hot tea. She had strapped his sprained ankle while he'd related the night's events.

'I'm gonna have to get going,' he concluded. 'I can't risk you falling foul of the law.'

She tutted. 'You aren't in any condition to travel. Besides, no one will know you're here. You'll be quite safe.'

'You were Billy's girlfriend. There's not much in this town the sheriff doesn't know. He'll be aware that we know each other. Won't be long before he comes a-knocking.'

'He might come asking questions but he's unlikely to search the place.' She shrugged. 'Even if he does, it's big enough for you to hide in.'

Branston chuckled and pointed to the clothes horse. 'In that case you'd better do something about that jacket and hat you're drying,' he chuckled. 'He might recognize them. They're his.'

'Oh, so I've got a thief on my hands as well, eh?' she smiled. 'Anyway, you can stay here as long as you like. At least until your ankle's better.'

'Jenny, I don't know what I'm going to do. I was planning on trying to make the ranch viable again. I've managed to get a basic crew around me. At the same time I could follow up my enquiries about Billy's death. Now....'

'You forget all that for the time being. I'll make up the spare bed. When you've warmed up you get some sleep. You need it.'

It was later. They had said their goodnights and Branston was lying between clean sheets. The smell of the snuffed candle beside his bed gave way to the delicate scent of lavender, reminding him it was a woman's house. He could hear her pottering about before retiring in the room the other side of the landing. Rain pattered against the window. The bed felt good but sleep wasn't coming come easy. Thoughts, images, questions irritatingly criss-crossed his mind. There was Billy's unsolved death. He himself was in trouble with the law. Wherever his mind poked there were riddles. Why was he sprung from the slammer? And by whom?

Suddenly he remembered the tattoo of a star on the back of one of the men's hands. He felt he'd seen that somewhere before. He thought he might have been set up to be shot while escaping, but he'd been wrong there. Then who the hell were his unknown benefactors?

It was a little after he'd heard the bed creak in Jenny's room, that a wave of adrenalin whooshed through his body as a thought targeted him from nowhere. 'Jenny!' he said in a raised voice. He wheezed in pain as he shifted himself into a sitting position.

'What is it?' she asked, coming through the door at the moment he lit the candle.

'I've just had the wildest thought.'

'What?'

He didn't answer but threw a question enigmatically back at her. 'Besides the Double B, is there anywhere in the locality that Billy might stay? Some place with which he was familiar and could hole up?'

'Billy? Hole up? What do you mean?'

'Is there a place?' he persisted.

She sat on the edge of the bed, feeling for his brow. 'I think your soaking's given you a chill. You're feverish.'

He pulled away from her touch. 'I don't think he could stay with folks. Everybody would be against him. But there might be a place. A hidden place.'

There was nothing extraordinary about the man's temperature so Jenny responded to him at the rational level, considering his words for what they meant. Then she said, 'One day Billy and I were having a picnic, on the range some ten miles north of the Double B. Late afternoon it began to rain.' She looked at the water-spattered window. 'As bad as it is now. Anyway, we found a cave, high up,in the rocks. Hidden from view for all intents and purposes. We sheltered there. The rain didn't stop before it got dark.' She looked coy. 'Billy lit a fire and we stayed overnight.' She looked up again. 'There. You're getting secrets out of me. Why do you ask?'

'I think Billy might be alive.'

She visibly started, then grabbed his hand. 'Alive? What do you mean? Why do you say that?'

'I told you there was a man in the shadows when the two strangers sprung me. It's been bugging me. For a split second I caught the glimmer of his face as he struck a match. It was dark, raining, and I was at the other side of the street. But there was something familiar about him. Something I couldn't put my finger on. The impression was so hazy. He was with the men. I know that because I looked back and caught sight of him joining them. There was a third horse standing by too. My mind has been so full of things I didn't think of it. But it just suddenly come to me. Jenny, it was Billy.'

She gripped his hand tighter. 'You sure?'

'No. But who else would be bothered to get me out of the hoosegow? I don't know anybody in these parts. In fact, folks hate me and the Branston name. And it makes sense. If Billy was in trouble, what better way of getting the law off his trail than getting folks to think he was dead. One thing Billy had – has – and that's a head on his shoulders.' He eased himself up a little. 'Did I tell you about the tattoo?'

'No.'

'One of the men tonight had a tattoo on the back of his hand. A star. Think I've see'd it someplace afore.'

'Luke's got a tattoo like that. You know Luke, one of Billy's friends.'

'That's it,' Branston grunted with satisfaction. 'I saw it at Billy's funeral.'

'Yes. Luke was there.'

'Jenny, it's coming together.'

'It's a crazy thought, Joe.'

'I know. Crazy enough to be true.' He thought some more. 'There's still bits missing, of course,' he said, excitement evident in his voice. 'But a picture's forming. Someone's gun-running to the Comanches and they've pinned it on Billy. Just like they've framed me with Meadows' murder. It'd be the same person. My money's on Drucker being behind it all. Arrogant empire-building bastard.'

Jenny cooled. 'I think things are getting's fanciful. There's still a lot that needs explaining.

If Billy were to be alive, like you say, who's that in his coffin in the cemetery?'

Branston chuckled. 'Doesn't have to be anyone. Broke as I am, if I had a thousand dollars I'd stake it all on that coffin being full of stones!'

EIGHTEEN

Branston slept till mid-morning. Hearing him rouse Jenny brought him a pot of tea. 'Figure a man can get a real liking for this stuff,' he said as he took his first sip.

'How's the invalid this fine morning?'

He looked at the window. 'Does "fine" mean the rain's stopped?'

'Yes. It has the promise of a beautiful day.'

He swung round, tried his foot gingerly on the floor and sucked in air.

'Ankle no better?' she observed.

'Good enough,' he said. 'Be better tonight when I go out to the cave. Can I borrow your horse?'

'It's not a saddle horse. Never had leather on its back. I'll take you out in the gig.'

'I've been thinking. This idea about Billy. Let's not raise our hopes. It's just a long shot.' He took some more tea. 'I'll take the gig out myself if that's agreeable to you?'

'It is not agreeable, Joe Branston. I will take the reins. You'll never find it by yourself in the dark and, anyway, I'm not missing out on this. Besides, you go alone you might be seen. I drive, you can hide under a blanket.'

'You got a gun?'

'Gun? Why would you want a firearm?'

'I'm a wanted man, Jenny. I would like some defence.'

'That could make matters worse if you are challenged.' She noted his resolute face. 'All right, suit yourself. Father had guns. I'll show you later. You're welcome to take your pick.' She left the room and, while he drank more tea, he heard her moving about. She returned with a black suit on a hanger and a bundle under her arm. 'They belonged to father. He was about your build but you'll have to pull the trousers in with a belt. You haven't got his stomach.' She laid the suit on the bed. 'Couldn't bring myself to throw them out. Haven't touched them since he died.' She sniffed at the shirt and miscellaneous items still in her hand. 'A trifle musty I'm afraid. However, you get dressed while I make breakfast.'

Minutes later he presented himself in the downstairs kitchen where bacon was already sizzling in a skillet. Used to range garb he felt awkward in formal clothing.

'There's shaving tackle there,' she said, pointing to a razor in a large china mug.

'Your father's again?' he asked, advancing to a mirror by the window and examining his stubble with his fingers.

'No,' she giggled. 'Billy's.' She caught his look as he turned from the mirror. 'Oh, Joe. Don't be shocked. We were adults.'

'Still can't stop thinking of Billy as a young kid.' He adjusted himself to the thought while he lathered up and began scraping his cheek. As he did so his eyes strayed from the mirror to the garden through the window. 'Jeez,' he breathed. The sheriff's hat and jacket along with his own trousers were pegged to the line. He dropped the razor and moved to the door, opening it slowly and glancing around to check he wasn't observed. Then, hobbling as fast as he could on his sprained ankle, he hauled the clothes down and returned.

'These could have been seen,' he said as he closed the door. He pushed the bundle into a cupboard. 'Even a pair of men's trousers could arouse suspicions.'

'Sorry, Joe. I remember you did warn me last night, but a woman tends to do these things automatically. They were still damp and I'd told you it was a fine morning. At least the back garden can't be seen from the trail.'

He completed his shaving and mopped his face as he settled into a chair before the plate of bacon, eggs and fried bread. He'd almost finished when there came a knock at the front door. The two looked at each other. He got to his feet and positioned himself behind the kitchen door, indicating with a silent gesture for her to answer.

He heard the boards creak as she crossed the house and opened the door. 'Morning, Miss Jenny.' He recognized the sheriff's voice.

'Good morning, Sheriff.'

'There's been a break-out from jail. Joe Branston.'

'Joe Branston,' she said putting surprise into her voice. 'Why were you holding him?'

'Chief suspect in the murder of Meadows the lawyer.'

'Mr Meadows dead? Oh, I didn't know.'

'Yes. Gut-shot with Branston's gun. Couldn't be more conclusive. You haven't seen anything?'

'No.'

'I don't think he got away on horseback and as far as my enquiries show there hasn't been a horse stolen so there's a chance he hasn't got far yet.'

There was a pause and then Branston heard him continue. 'His brother was courting you and I know you've met Branston since he's taken over the Double B. He's desperate and might contact you.'

'He hasn't been here, Sheriff.'

'You'd tell me if he did show?'

'Of course.'

There was a long 'Mmmmm'. Then, 'Well, miss, you've got some outbuildings here. You never know. Mind if I look around?'

'No, of course. Anything to help.'

Branston heard the door close and feet crunching on gravel outside. He realized from his position behind the door he could be seen from the window. He ducked down behind a large wash tub. Jenny came through, silently noting Branston's hiding place. She opened the kitchen door and stood in the doorway. With the door open Branston could hear footsteps and squeaking hinges as shed doors were opened.

'Doesn't seem to be here,' he heard the sheriff say after a spell. 'You let us know if you see or hear anything suspicious, Miss Jenny. You know it's an offence to help a wanted man. You being a judge's daughter and all, you'd know there could be serious consequences.'

'Of course, Sheriff.'

After a while, he heard Jenny close the door. 'He's gone,' she shouted back. 'I can see him riding back to town with his deputy.'

'He's right, you know,' Branston said when she rejoined him. 'You could be in trouble helping me.'

She smiled. 'Like I said before, we're grown people.'

Branston got to his feet. 'I'll hide away upstairs until it's dark.'

NINETEEN

It was well past midnight and some time had elapsed since they had heard the last of the revellers from the saloon passing the house. Branston had checked the judge's two hand-guns and pushed them into his belt. He harnessed the horse to the gig and climbed inside the carriage. Jenny laid a blanket over him and then strolled in the moonlight to the fence to check there was no one on the trail. A few lights were visible from the nearby town, but no sounds.

She quietly flicked the ribbons and the carriage rolled on to the trail. Once well clear of the town, Branston pulled away the blanket and sat beside her. For most of the journey they didn't speak. Neither knew exactly what to expect and whatever could be said had been said. It was around three that the black shape of a rock formation loomed up ahead, like a massive ship on the dark sea of the range.

Jenny reined in at the foot. 'See that gap in the rocks,' she said, pointing. 'You can just about see it.' She raised her pointed finger and swung her arm as though drawing a picture. 'It's a means of access to the cave, way up there.'

Branston eased himself out of the carriage and handed her one of the guns. 'Keep that ready. You never know what could happen out in the middle of nowhere this time of the morning.'

'I'm coming with you, Joe.'

'Oh, no, you're not,' he said, ground-hitching the horse. His eyes scanned the edifice. He could just make out the darkened hole way above amongst the rocks.

'Very well, I'll stay. But watch your step, Joe. The gap is very narrow in places, difficult to get by. That's why it would be such a good place for anyone to hide in.'

'Keep looking and listening,' he said as he headed for the gap. Slowly he made his way upwards, having to feel his way ahead for the most part. Now and again his feet crunched on scree. The increasing bite in the breeze told him he was gaining height. The irregular ground and the requirement of moving upward was no friend to his sprained joint. Suddenly a slug spanged off a boulder near him and he dropped to the ground.

'Don't come any closer,' someone shouted. 'It might be dark but I got a better view from up here than you.' It was unmistakably the voice of his brother. A wave of feeling washed through Branston's system with the recognition.

'It's me. Joe.'

'Joe?'

'Yeah, your damn brother.'

'Jesus, what the hell you doing out here?' Billy yelled. Then, 'You brought the law?' he queried. 'They couldn't get to me otherwise. Only Jenny and me knew about the cave.'

'Christ, you know me better than that, don't you, kid? Jenny told me about the cave. I had to see you.'

There was a long pause. 'Come on up then.'

In the darkness at the cave entrance they embraced, long and silently. Then Billy led the way in, a short distance to where there was a low fire, just beyond a turning such that its light couldn't be seen from outside. 'Billy, it's really you,' Branston said. 'I thought you were dead.'

'So does everyone else, I hope. How did you find out?'

'Didn't. Just put two and two together and guessed ... and hoped. 'Specially when I got sprung. There was nobody who'd do that 'ceptin' you. Then I figure I saw you in the shadows that night. In the darkness lighting a cheroot. Wasn't sure. Could have been a trick of the light. I can see now it wasn't.'

Billy chuckled. 'Yeah, it was me, all right. Couldn't miss the opportunity to have a look at my big brother again. Even if it was only as he skedaddled down a dark street with his tail between his legs.'

'You ain't gonna be safe here for long. The stink I been kicking up I wouldn't be surprised if it ain't long before the sheriff's opening up your grave. Even if he doesn't, other folks might guess you ain't dead, just like I did.'

'Well, until that happens this place will be as good as any other for me.'

They both hunkered down before the fire. 'You got some sidekicks, ain't yuh?' Branston said casting his eyes around the fire-lit cave but seeing no one else. 'Clem and Luke, ain't it?. The guys that sprung me. They here?'

'Nope. Out arranging a job. Now my ranching days are over, I gotta live by my wits. I'm still learning but the boys have been in the game for a long time. When it's fixed up we move out.'

'Does that mean another law-breaking caper?'

Billy chuckled again. 'The less you know the better. You're in enough trouble already without being an accessory.'

'Is there some way outa this mess, Billy?'

'It's the way the cards have been dealt.'

'Who's in the grave?' Branston asked after a spell.

'You wouldn't know him. Kid called Dave Harleyson.'

'What? You didn't kill him?'

'Let's say he obliged me by dying at a convenient time.'

'That don't answer my question.'

Billy shook his head. 'No, I didn't kill him. He was trying to break one of the horses and fell bad. It was a genuine accident. Poor kid died almost instantly. I knew the law were on to me and were just waiting their chance. To complicate things poor old Dave kicks the bucket. It was when we were deciding to bring him into town that I had the idea of getting the boys to pass him off as me. I was the one the law were really after, not Clem and Luke. Least not on this state. They've kept so low in these parts nobody's got much idea what they look like. 'Ceptin' Jenny, of course.'

'It was wrong to use his body that way, Billy. The lad had got a mother up in Buckler's Creek.'

'Everybody's had a mother some time, some place.' Billy's one eye appraised his elder brother. 'Still the Puritan, eh, Joe? Listen, it was all in a good cause. I needed somebody in the box.'

Branston's face hardened. 'I sure am learning a lot, Billy. The sheriff was right. It was me who was the mug.'

'What does that mean?'

'Something he said way back when I first rode into town. Said I didn't know you. He was sure-as-hell right on that. He's been right about a lot of things.' He pondered. 'What about the doctor? Did he know it wasn't you when he made out the death certificate?'

'We made the body look like it might have been mine. Put one of my black patches over Dave's eye. We left it till late at night, knowing the doc would have been drinking. He'd never met me and could hardly stand when the boys took the body in. Despite that we reckon he could still be suspicious. Mind he wasn't above taking a couple of hundred dollars not to ask any questions.'

'What about the coroner and Meadows?'

'They took the doc's word for it. The coroner hadn't seen me before. Meadows had but he didn't see the body. But, like the doc, he suspected so we paid him off too.'

'How come they died?'

'That was the boys. A mite over-zealous. I'd left the territory for a spell and they was acting in what they thought was my best interests. See, your asking questions unsettled the old guys. One of 'em might have cracked. The boys paid the doc a visit, just to remind him not to cause any trouble.

They're a couple of rough *hombres* and it seems he had a heart attack. Natural causes really.'

'And Meadows?'

'Yes, the lads were wrong there. I'll admit that. Not in killing him but in framing you. As I said, he knew about the ruse. In fact, I figured it could be useful having someone in town who knew. Could help to throw folk off the scent mebbe if necessary. He was paid well. Trouble was the greedy skunk wanted more. Put the squeeze on Clem and Luke while I was away. It was their scatter-brained idea to frame you at the same time, just to get you to stop asking damn questions. When I came back and learned you were in the slammer I told them they had to get you out. Made sure they did too. That's one of the reasons I was there. The sheriff would have recognized me if I'd done the job myself. Ain't no way of disguising a patch!'

'And was that your boys taking pot-shots at me north of the pasture?'

Billy chuckled. 'Yeah. They didn't know what to do. I was away trying to fix some business and you turns up out of the blue, asking questions, stirring folk, making 'em think. We wanted sleeping dogs left sleeping. They thought the best thing was to try to scare you off. They knew better than to have harmed you, you being my brother and all.'

'And I thought it was Drucker behind it all.'

'No, Joe. He's as straight as they come.'

Branston shook his head cynically. 'I rode into his place and virtually accused him of killing you and trying to kill me.'

Billy laughed again. 'I'd liked to have seen that.'

'Jeez, Billy, I can't believe all this.'

The youngster chuckled. 'You ain't changed, Joe.'

'You ain't always been a bad 'un. When did it start?'

'I started out quite legit. See, for years the government procured horses under what was called the contract system. That meant the purchasing for the whole army was done through Washington. The upshot was poor quality at a high price: $120 for a $60 brute. Well, the pen-pushers handling the government budget got cost-conscious. Reckon the new administration had gone through Washington with a clean broom. Anyways, they allowed some regiments to buy their own horseflesh as an experiment. For them it meant better mounts and opened up local markets for someone with drive and business sense. That's where I came in. Minimized labour and overheads, worked like a buck nigger so that I could offer top dollar stock for a bottom dollar price. Made losses for a spell then it began to pay off. Would you believe it, Joe? Your little Billy Patch cornered the market in the territory! Eventually it began paying off real big dividends. I bought the spread in Brightwater. No mortgage. Straight cash. Started to expand. Then thought of you naturally. You remember I sent you come-on letters?'

Branston rubbed his chin. 'Yeah. I remember. Never took 'em up.'

'You should have done. Then none of this might have happened. Why the hell did you leave it so late?'

'Didn't want to come at first because of pride.

Then things went from bad to worse for me and I thought what the hell's wrong in working for my kid brother anyhow?'

'You were always the one to drag his feet.'

'Anyway, what happened?'

'Well, you know me. Quick-fire temper. Could have done with you around a mite quicker. You always was as steady as a rock. I needed counterbalancing. Anyways, had an argument with some army man in a saloon in Houston. The bozo didn't like the way I handled him. We exchanged a few punches then he drags his bloody nose off into the darkness and I never see'd hide nor hair of him again. But, Jeez, he must have had some pull 'cos the next thing I know I've lost the army contract. I pushed, even went to see the top brass, but no dice. Reckon I got put on the army blacklist for good an' all.

'Well, the only outlet here for horses on any scale is the military. With the main outlet blocked, the business went down an' down. Started losing hand over fist. Laid off men, ran down the stock. You know the rest.'

'I don't.'

'Well, what would you have done? I turned my hand to anything. Anything that would bring in a dollar. Animal feed, farm implements.'

'But why guns, Billy?'

'Listen, big brother. When you're in business you make all kinds of contacts. All kinda folk, all kinda goods. This guy had a shipment of Winchesters he wanted getting shed of fast. Fast meant cheap. But they was as hot as a skillet on a camp-fire so I couldn't go hawking 'em around, could I? Just sold 'em to willing buyers. That's business, Joe.'

'Didn't you give no mind to what they'd be used for?'

'Nope, 'ceptin' they maybe might be used to give the army some trouble. That didn't upset me none. Not after the way they'd treated me.'

'The weapons were used against ordinary folks, Billy. Women and kids.'

Billy paused. 'Yes, I know. That was bad. But judgement like that is hindsight, ain't it?'

'You put me in a spot, kid.'

Billy chuckled. 'Why?'

'Well, for the past couple of weeks I've been trying to prove your innocence. Now, look at the situation I'm in. You weren't my kid brother, it'd be my duty to take you in.'

Billy mock-punched his shoulder. 'You'll never change. It ain't gonna get you nowhere, being up to the eyeballs in principles.' He laughed. 'A guy can drown in principles.'

'I know that but I'm too old to change.'

'Listen, Joe. We got you into this mess. As you're here, you may as well hole up with us. When the boys get back, we'll find a way of letting the law know you didn't kill Meadows.'

'Staying here will just get me in deeper. I'll go back and try to get out of the mess myself.' He studied the fire a spell. 'Listen, anything Jenny can get you while you're holed up? Food?'

'She's here? God, I'll have to see her.'

'She's in the gig at the foot of the rocks.'

'I love that gal but it'd be wrong to involve her in

any of this. I'm gonna have to disappear for good and proper soon. But I have to see her one more time.' He rose and began to walk back to the cave entrance. Branston followed him. 'Stay here,' the elder said as they neared the moonlight. 'I'll send her up.'

'When you get her back to town, make sure you convince her not to come out here again. Be too risky. If folks are close to guessing the truth then the sheriff will be watching her once he knows I ain't as dead as he hoped. 'Sides we got enough chow here. It was part of my plan to hole up here for quite a piece. Robinson Crusoe didn't have nothin' on our set-up here.'

'You sure there's nothing I can do for you, Billy. I feel so helpless.'

'Don't you worry yourself none on my account, Joe. You got enough troubles of your own. Billy Patch can look after himself. Just you make a go of that ranch when you've shucked the Meadows charge. It's yours now.'

There was a lump in Joe Branston's throat as they embraced again. 'OK, kid. So long,' he said making his way out of the entrance. As he began to move down the slope he turned to see the slight figure of his brother emerge from the shadows above him. 'Couldn't resist one last look at my big bozo of a brother,' the younger one shouted. 'Maybe our paths will cross again. So help me, I sure hope so.' His hand rose. 'So long, Joe.'

A muzzle flash briefly lit up the scene, a thundering crack echoed in the darkness and the small figure pitched forward, riffling the scree until he lay crumpled at Branston's' feet. Branston dropped to his knees, his hands exploring the form. His kid brother was dead.

TWENTY

He whirled round. 'Sheriff?' he challenged savagely.

'Nope.'

Branston's gun had already come out and his eyes and barrel probed the blackness. The shot had been fired from the side. The voice continued, 'You can't see me. But I can see you and my gun is aimed at your vitals. So be sensible and drop it.'

Branston's pistol hit the scree noisily. Then, from the shadows near the cave entrance, a figure emerged. Branston hadn't recognized the voice and he didn't recognize the man.

'Who the hell are you?' Branston shouted. 'Law?'

'You could say that. Name's Sinclair. Lieutenant Joel Sinclair, Rangers.'

'Rangers? Don't see no badge,' Branston commented as the man approached and he got a better look.

'I ain't on duty at this present time,' Sinclair said as he moved closer. 'If you know your weapons, mister, and look close you'll see this is a Rangers-issue Paterson I've got trained on your belly.'

'What the hell's this business to do with you? That's my brother you've killed.'

'That brother of your'n put us in the way of a nasty job. Facing up to Comanches who had been slaughtering white settlers with shiny new Winchesters supplied by the man known as Billy Patch. My best friend had his head smashed away by one of them.' He moved up, his gun automatically keeping level on Branston's stomach, and he took a closer look at the still figure. 'He took a lotta tracking. Vowed I'd get him and I did.' Triumph was plain in his voice.

'That wasn't the smartest thing to do, fella,' Branston said. 'Especially for a Rangers man. There's two other desperadoes about. They could have heard the shot and blasted you to hell. How come you're out here anyways?'

'Followed you and the girl.'

Branston grunted cynically. 'The blind leading the blind. We weren't sure my brother was alive. Or that he was out here.'

'You were playing a long shot. So was I.'

'She OK down there?' Branston asked.

'Yeah.'

Paying no more heed to the threatening pistol, Branston picked up his own and holstered it. 'How come you were tailing us?'

'Been around town a spell. Like you I figured there was something fishy going on. I had no other leads so I hung around. I was out near the girl's this morning before the sheriff came. Saw her put a man's duds on the line. Wondered how come a woman who lives alone is putting out a man's trousers. Could be innocent but I'd learned you'd broken jail and the law was drawing a blank on your whereat. Then, after spying the clothes on the line, I see you rush out and take 'em down.'

'Why didn't you do something about it then?'

'When you ain't sure about what's going on, it pays to lay back and watch.'

Branston bent over his brother. 'Do me a favour. Help me down with him.'

Suddenly there was a cry from below. 'Joe! Billy!' It was Jenny's voice.

Branston took out his pistol and began to hobble down the slope. When he and Sinclair reached the bottom they could see Jenny sitting in the gig. A man was gripping her collar with a gun held against her head.

'Billy's sidekicks,' Branston muttered.

'We've got the girl, stranger,' the one in the gig said. 'We're gonna light out. You follow us and you'll find her dead body on the trail. Now drop your gun, stranger. And you, Branston.'

Neither man moved.

'You use those irons and the girl dies.'

Sinclair and Branston tossed their weapons aside. While the one man kept them covered the other dropped down from the gig. He unfastened the horse from the traces and hit its flank so that it shot off into the darkness. Then he led one of the saddled horses to the gig. 'Mount up, miss.'

'You wouldn't use me as a hostage, would you, Luke?' she said. 'This is Jenny, Billy's girl.'

'I know but things change, miss. Do as I say.'

'May as well shoot me now,' Sinclair said defiantly. 'I ain't gonna give up your trail. And if you do shoot me, there'll be another, and another. The

Rangers won't let you go.'

The man hefted his gun threateningly. 'Don't spur me, Ranger.'

Jenny made to disembark but suddenly there was a bang and the scene briefly lit up like a stage show. Billy Patch, smoking gun in hand, was leaning crazy-fashion against a rock to the rear of his brother. The man called Luke staggered, fired, and for a moment it was dark again.

Sinclair dropped and rolled with slugs from the second man spanging off the boulders behind him. His own gun came up. From a prone position, he fired twice and the second man collapsed.

Branston had retrieved his own gun and hobbled over to the two men in turn. They were dead. By the time he'd got to Billy, Jenny was cradling his brother's head in her arms. She was sobbing. 'Oh, Joe. He's gone.'

TWENTY-ONE

They returned to the ranch with the three bodies on the buckboard, the lieutenant riding alongside. Nobody had chance to sleep and it was soon light. With his sprained leg Branston couldn't yet manage to wield a shovel properly so Hogan and the *vaqueros* helped him dig a grave out under a tree on the northern pasture and Billy Patch was buried yet again: for sure this time. Branston had hammered in the rough marker he had made back at the ranch and, bathed in the light of dawn, they had stood in silence with their thoughts.

Then the group rode into town with the bodies of the two hardcases. Sinclair reported to the sheriff what he'd heard of the conversation between Billy and his brother. He'd been at the cave entrance and heard it all. The sheriff accepted the final explanation of events and Branston was cleared of the murder charge. The bodies were lodged with the coroner and Sinclair then headed back to his unit.

A couple of days passed and Branston was in the Law Office tying up a few loose ends for the sheriff's report.

'Don't take it so bad about Billy,' the sheriff

mouthed after the business was concluded. 'Deep down your brother was a bad 'un.'

'Oh, no,' Branston countered. 'You didn't know him like I did. There was some good in him. Once. He just lost it somewhere along the trail. But when and where, I can't guess.'

'Well, take solace in the fact that what happened to him was inevitable,' the sheriff persisted pompously. 'He fell foul of the law.'

Branston sniffed contemptuously. 'Garbage.' He still didn't like the lawman even though in the event the officer had been acting properly throughout. 'Oh, I ain't defending what he did. But the law is merely an expediency. Even at its best, judgement is crude and brutal because when the chips are down it's merely a simplification. A damned, convenient simplification that makes money for the ones that designed it and manage to rig themselves a place in running it.'

The sheriff went to speak again but Branston had hobbled out without giving him the chance.

Jenny was waiting for him outside. He'd decided to stay on at the ranch and one of his first tasks after the burial of his brother had been to apologize to Drucker for his suspicions. The matter-of-fact cattle owner had just shrugged and slapped him on the shoulder. 'You're inexperienced in many ways, Branston,' he had said with a chuckle. 'Not the least in business. You want any help or advice in that direction, you know where I am.'

Once the truth was out, Drucker's sentiments were echoed amongst the rest of the community and folks were already mellowing towards the new horse-rancher. Back in town he'd found no problem in getting bank funding and dealing with local traders.

And, once again, he'd promised himself he'd seen the last of the booze. Come hell or high water, this time he was going to stand by it.

On the Law Office porch he put his arm around Jenny's shoulder. 'Thanks for your help,' he said. Earlier that morning she had taken him out in her gig so that he could make his apologies to Drucker. 'You know,' he went on, 'it'd real pleasure me to see you on a more regular basis. I think you know that, Jenny.'

But his heart fell when, in an elaborate gesture, she took the arm from around her shoulder. He felt real despondent until he became aware that she had retained an extraordinary tight grip on his hand. That gave him some comfort.

They stood that way for a time, unstated feelings in their touch. 'Yes, I would like that,' she said eventually. 'But don't expect anything more yet awhiles. Don't rush things, Joe. I loved your brother.'

He paused before speaking again. 'Me, too.' There was weakness in his voice.

Her face drawn, she squeezed his hand even more. 'And it is going to take me a long time to get over him.'

He looked up at the clouds and breathed deep. 'I never will.'